BEAUTIFUL ONE

AN LGBT HISTORICAL ROMANCE

USA TODAY BESTSELLING AUTHOR
KERRY ADRIENNE

Beautiful One
Kerry Adrienne
Beautiful One © 2019 Kerry Adrienne

All rights reserved under the International and Pan-American Copyright Conventions. No part of this book may be reproduced or transmitted in any form or by any means, electronic or mechanical, including photocopying, recording, or by any information storage and retrieval system, without permission in writing from the publisher.

This is a work of fiction. Names, places, characters and incidents are either the product of the author's imagination or are used fictitiously, and any resemblance to any actual persons, living or dead, organizations, events or locales is entirely coincidental.

Many thanks to:

Cover Design by Covers by Combs

Editing by Grace Bradley Editing, LLC

I count him braver who overcomes his desires than him who conquers his enemies, for the hardest victory is over the self
−Aristotle

ONE

Kallistos nodded toward the people gathered on the sides of the street to see the parade. A bubble of sound erupted as dancers floated by beside him, pushing him along the route in a wall of sound and motion.

"You'll do fine. They love to see heroes die." Stephanos shot him a look that was part disgust, part something inscrutable.

"As long as they die well." Kallistos raised his voice to compete with the noise. Chimes rang around him and *aulos* music cut through the air as he hurried to keep in step with Stephanos. Baking bread's sweet, thick aroma wafted over the crowd and combined with the rich scent of wine fresh from the countryside. His stomach gurgled.

The Great Dionysia, the largest festival of the year, would open with a feast unlike any he'd ever seen, or so Stephanos had said. Charred, spit-cooked meats sent columns of oily smoke into the air, beckoning him with hazy tendrils. He dragged in a long sniff, closing his eyes to savor the laden air.

"It's a magnificent part, one worthy of the gods' admiration. You wrote it well and will play it well on stage." Stephanos shook the ornate phallic pole in response to the acclamation and the skitter of beads along the wooden shaft sent a chill up Kallistos's arms. "Everyone will love you."

"I hope so." Kallistos scanned the crowd. He'd never seen so many people in one place before.

Hordes of citizens, many wearing red and carrying wooden bowls of bread, fresh laurel leaves, and sharp incense pushed along with them in the parade. Peals of laughter sang through the crowd as children chased each other along the sidelines and young women held hands and danced, their hair free and loose in the wind.

"I have every faith in you." Stephanos hit the pole on the earthen roadway as he walked, thumping it in time with the chants from the crowd.

They'd reach the temple soon, and everyone sensed the excitement of the moment, their movements becoming more frenetic with each step closer to the holy place.

"Sophocles will be a challenge." Kallistos waved, forcing a smile. The dancers jingled small metal bells as they moved, and the flutists trilled like twittering birds. A slight headache pounded in his temples, surely the result of little food, bright sunlight, and loud noise. The temple would be a respite.

"We can beat the old man."

"With your support." Truer words he hadn't spoken before. Without Stephanos, he'd not likely even be in Athens, much less in the city participating in the festival. His benefactor knew it, and yet still held faith in him.

"You have it. I've invested a lot in you." Stephanos pulled his deep-red tunic closer and banged the pole on the ground. His cropped hair, graying at the sides, was held clipped in laurel leaves and small flowers in a band around the crown of his head. "But know this well. A loss will come at a great cost to me."

"I'll do my best to not let you down." Kallistos adjusted the ivy necklace that trailed around his neck and hung to his knees. He'd be lying if he said he wasn't concerned. If he lost, his entire career would be over before it really started. The only playwrights that got a second chance were those who could fund their own art or were friends with someone who could afford to fund the frivolities of words.

A young dancer swept by him, her gown floating around her ankles as she moved, flower petals dropping from the basket she slung over her forearm. She slid the tips of her fingers down his arm, raising the hairs in an electric touch before dancing on ahead to circle others in the parade. Kallistos watched her move and undulate as rapture played across her features.

He knew he was fortunate. The archon, the appointed leader of the Great Dionysia festival, had chosen the perfect benefactor for his plays. Wealthy. Strong. And someone who didn't meddle in the creative aspects of writing and producing a drama. Each playwright participating in the festival was assigned a benefactor, and the Fates had smiled on him. There was no one he'd rather have than Stephanos.

The crowd stomped and catcalled in a surge of sound and Kallistos turned to see what caused their excitement. Movement behind him came in a great wave and the parade threatened to collapse onto itself as spectators joined the revelers in the street.

"Sophocles." Stephanos spat on the ground.

"Damn old man." He picked up his pace. "I can't wait to see him lose."

Kallistos jogged to catch up. "May Dionysus reward our hard work."

Stephanos nodded, setting his jaw like a fortress as he forged on toward the temple. "May Dionysus smite that son of a bitch."

"May he." Kallistos held back a grin. Gods willing, they'd be at Dionysus's temple soon. The god of the vine oversaw the festival, and throughout the whole event, wine flowed freely in his honor.

"May your great horse surprise the old man and dry up his thoughts." Stephanos grinned.

"May the gods hear your plea."

"May your tragedies ignite the crowd's tears."

Mouth suddenly dry, Kallistos took in a deep breath. His tragedies were strong, and if he was chosen to perform his satyr play, he held a good chance of defeating the old playwright. At worst, the satyr play was passable, and at best, possibly brilliant if the actors got their timing down. When he'd written it, all the pieces came together like the solution to the most complex and perfect puzzle, but when he'd had actors perform it, the pieces fell apart like so many shells on the beach.

Though it was difficult to write, direct, and act in a

set of plays, he welcomed the challenge. Sophocles had done it many times and he always impressed the crowd with his ability to handle everything. By far, he was the favorite to win in Athens, and besting him would take more than skill, dumb luck, and a few good plays. It'd also take strong political backing and a nod from the gods. Kallistos watched his sure-footed benefactor urge the crowd into applause. Stephanos carried little doubt that he backed the strongest plays in the festival.

If only he had the same confidence Stephanos had. Kallistos figured himself more of a realist. Even getting a coveted position in performance order wouldn't guarantee a win. No, in order to take the festival prize, everything would have to be magnificent, from inception to final call, including his own schmoozing of those in important positions. The gods' favor was beyond his control.

He shook his head as acid bubbled in his gut. He hated fake campaigning for support. In fact, he hated dealing with people at all unless he was directing them—when he could tell the actors what to do and how to best do it, like figures on a stick. Otherwise, he preferred to be alone with his thoughts.

He held his palms out to greet the onlookers as Stephanos had guided, and they waved in return. A thousand smiles surrounded him, and his heart thudded as excitement pushed away his nervousness.

After this festival, everyone in Athens will know who I am. They will know my plays. And when I'm rich, I can hide away and write as I wish. Someone else can face the public for me then. I won't be like Sophocles with a harem of followers begging to wash my feet. He longed to rush away, abandon the parade for a smaller gathering. His actors and their costumes and lines awaited his direction, and he couldn't wait to get back to them.

As the procession passed the market area where the square opened wide, the crowd danced and chanted even more wildly. Banners flung themselves in the breezy sunshine and women tossed colorful floral wreaths toward the giant statue of Dionysus as it rolled down the earthen road toward his temple. Everywhere Kallistos looked, people lifted wine skins and cups in honor of the god. If wine could have flowed in the streets like rivers of red, Athens would have made it happen. No expense was too great for the largest festival of the year.

"Smile, Kallistos! Act! They clamor for you." Stephanos held the staff high, waving it in the air. "Play the part the gods have granted you."

"Maybe they clamor for my head." He fought the urge to duck and run into a near alley.

"Your pretty head will be the face of Athens in a few days, so get used to the attention."

Kallistos's face warmed. People always sought to be near him because of his looks, but he wanted to be known for more than a supposedly handsome visage. The birthing pangs of creation split him wide and he needed to make people's guts twist with the wrenching of loss, and the solitary agony of love unrequited. His natal duty was to thrust into their imaginations the burn of the sword parting flesh and the tight grip of lust swarming their loins. *Theater*. His one true love. Never would he allow himself to bow to the shallowness of celebrity, mundane chatter, and the frivolity of looks.

No, if his plays couldn't speak for him, he'd rather be mute.

A gaggle of temple virgins sashayed past, baskets of bread and fruit on their heads and long, tight braids swinging below their waists, hitting their bottoms like full drums. Behind them, people filled in every spot in the square as the parade slowed. *Aulos* melodies drowned the air with syrupy chords reflected in rising choruses of young boys chanting as the large statue of Dionysus was pushed up the final hill to the temple where it would sit until it was moved to the *theatron* at dawn. Furred and crowned priests raised their phallic poles in celebratory angst, the spirals of their long goat-horned helmets piercing the moment.

The statue halted in front of the temple, creaking on its wheeled base, and the crowd circled the wooden god in a swarm of prostration. Men, women, and children alike bowed to the effigy and sang songs and made promises of worship.

Kallistos trudged forward. *Almost done.* Soon, he'd perform his plays for the citizens of Athens and the parade would be forgotten as a stray thread in the long cloth of memory.

"I'll meet you tonight." Stephanos gripped his arm. "I've got to go talk to the judges' group. Make them love you even more now that they've seen your golden hair and poet's eyes. I'll have them lapping at my heels like stray beasts in search of information on you and your plays."

Kallistos rolled his eyes and pulled free. "Surely you need me to come along as a token in this fantasy."

Stephanos shook his head. "No, I want to keep them guessing. They've gotten a glimpse of you now and I'm sure they have questions."

"Make them wait."

"Don't worry, I won't tell them anything. We're going to surprise everyone. Athens has never seen such a brilliant performance." Stephanos nodded his goodbye, raised his stick in salute, and disappeared into the mass of people lining the square.

Kallistos dropped back from the crowd, letting those behind him filter on ahead. The crowd moved as one now. One crazy crush of humanity reveling in a haze of wine, excitement, and religion. And more wine. Feverish revelers shouted and danced and drank while drummers thumped their wooden drums with smoothed sticks. Vendors of every type rolled out their wares in the market and cast lots to force a profit. Dionysus was well loved, and the celebration would last for days. The offerings of sacrifice—both bloody and bloodless, would show the love and respect everyone had for the god.

Kallistos sidestepped the frenzy and scanned the crowd. His place in the parade had afforded him a close spot to the statue, but people continued filling in the empty spaces as he waited and now the statue was surrounded by people standing, dancing, and praying. How soon could he leave without being considered disrespectful? The tall, wooden statue towered over the courtyard, casting a shadow over the crowd. The god, holding a fennel stick topped with a silvery pinecone, smiled at the mortals beneath him—his androgynous figure both soft and muscled. Kallistos shielded his eyes. *Please, oh great god, bless me with a win.* The sun glinted off the painted jeweled necklace like a wink.

He panned the crowd for an escape route and his gaze landed on a man staring right back at him. Frozen like a marble statue and dappled in the shady lowlights of the temple shadows, he looked directly at Kallistos. His broad shoulders curved with firm, smooth muscle. Wavy, dark hair teased his shoulders, curling just below the edge of muscle, and fine cheekbones rose above his solid jawline, chiseled and refined. *So kissable.* Kallistos shivered and dipped his head a moment. The man smiled and disappeared as a passerby moved in front of him.

In a moment, he was gone

ALEXIOS BACKED AWAY from view and clutched his crisp ivy necklace. Sophocles had not told him that Kallistos would be so handsome—perhaps the job would not be so difficult, after all. The quiet man in the shadow of Dionysus had to have been the playwright everyone was talking about—there were few

Greeks with sunlit hair, and he walked as part of the processional, beside Stephanos. It had to be him. Even from the distance, he was sure he saw the man's green eyes.

Indeed, he was the beautiful one.

The man Sophocles feared.

The flute music stopped, and the *archon's* voice echoed off the buildings surrounding the courtyard. Alexios brushed off the back of his *chiton* and stepped into the crowd, dodging revelers. Athenians of every social class vied for position to be near the *archon* and some shoved and elbowed to get closer to the small, elevated platform where he stood. Even slaves and prisoners who had been released in time to enjoy the festival pushed to hear the word that the City Dionysia had officially begun.

The *archon* held the city's breath in his hand.

Alexios pressed as close as he dared, hoping to catch a glimpse of Kallistos without being spotted. He wasn't ready to face him, but he hoped to gain a little information before he talked to him. Figuring out how to deal with the beautiful one was going to be a challenge—one he was more than excited about, now that he'd seen the man.

The crowd pressed tight and Alexios folded his arms to claim the space near him. Kallistos wasn't in sight, but he had to be near. Everyone would listen to the *archon's* speech.

"The City Dionysia is here again. Tonight, we dance," the *archon* shouted over the crowd.

A shriek of joy rose from the crowd and the *archon* waited for quiet before continuing.

"Tomorrow morning at sunrise, we convene in the *theatron* to pay tribute to the greatest city, Athens. The play competition will begin, and we'll feast and drink to Dionysus, most benevolent."

The crowd stomped its feet and yelled.

The *theatron*. Where dreams lived and died in the magical crush of a few precious hours. A place where one could pursue anything or be anyone. A place Alexios wanted to be—on stage for all to see. He longed to move men to tears. To fill their hearts with rage, and loneliness, and joy, and love.

He swallowed his emotion. Many nights in the fields while watching over the sheep, he'd fantasized about becoming a great actor performing in Athens—studying under the most powerful and influential playwright alive, the great Sophocles.

And now he worked for the great Sophocles, and it was his chance to make it out of the audience and onto the stage. And possibly, if everything went well, make a living doing what his heart desired. Sophocles was well rumored to be generous with his wealth if he found an actor worthy.

I can't fail. I won't.

Whatever it took, he'd make sure Sophocles won, and perhaps then win the great playwright's favor.

The *archon* went on about the great year Athens had, and the tribute wealth that would be deposited in the theater at daybreak. The gods would be proud, he said.

Alexios tuned out and searched for Kallistos among the meadow of dark-haired men. He wasn't visible anywhere in Alexios's sight. He was in the crowd, no doubt, and Alexios would find him eventually, though he wasn't in a rush. Though he wanted to please Sophocles, he wasn't yet sure how he'd carry out his task.

Athens would party in the streets for most of the night, then everyone would convene in the theater at dawn. He'd find Kallistos. And his journey to rule the stage would begin.

Kallistos wasn't in sight and a measure of relief washed over Alexios. The plan had to be orchestrated without a bumble or missed mark. His first major acting part—and Sophocles was his director. How many men would give up everything for the chance he now held?

"Let the festival begin," the *archon* said. Music played from every corner of the temple square and a flurry of doves beat the air with a million soft feathers, fluttering into the sky in a burst of cooing and motion.

A bump knocked him off guard and before he could recover his footing, a hand snaked around his hips and tugged him backward.

Alexios tried to free himself but the hold tightened. "What are you doing?"

"Did you fear I'd steal your jewels?" The squat man spoke close to his ear. "I've seen them before, and I dare say they are fine, if a little large, but not what I'm interested in. At least, not today." Wine stains splashed down the front of his red tunic and his unshaven face looked smudged with dirt.

"Mattan. You're a dirty pig." Alexios broke from the man's grip. "Don't touch me. I mean it."

"But you're touchy. Delectable." He licked his lips.

"Why are you here?" No way Kallistos would want to talk to him with Mattan hanging around. Sophocles's ever-present helper was nothing more than a crooked fool, though he couldn't see why. Sophocles held him in high regard, so the man must do something well, even if it was something unenviable.

"I'm here getting a jump out of you." Mattan smiled, his missing teeth sending flecks of spit into the air as he talked. "It worked."

Alexios stepped back, the heat of embarrassment climbing up his neck and making his cheeks burn. "I warn you for the final time. Keep your hands off me."

He scanned the market to make sure no one was watching. The crowd had begun to move away from the *archon's* platform and into the market to get food and drink with no sign they had seen Mattan's grasp.

Thank the gods.

The low rumble from everyone talking vibrated the air and the sun's rays split across the open space in a dance of brightness.

Mattan ran a fingertip across Alexios's arm. "You are so hard. And yet…so soft."

"Stop." He yanked his arm away. If Mattan weren't working for Sophocles too, he'd walk away. He'd have to put up with him.

"I can wait. But for now, Sophocles wants an update on the situation. Did you talk to the playwright?"

A cold streak sliced through Alexios's chest and he pushed his ivy necklace away from his chin.

Sophocles inspired most people but scared him witless. With no more than a breath, the old man could shatter a career before it had even begun. Sophocles was his chance to be on stage, and Alexios knew he'd better perform the task up to expectations, or else.

"Follow me," Alexios motioned, "we can't talk here."

Mattan leered. "Privacy. That's more like it. Lead on."

Alexios pushed his way toward the temple front, dodging sloshing wine bowls and near-drunk Athenians. Wouldn't be long until they'd be all-out drunk. That's how the festival went. A boys' chorus chanted a *dithramb* at the foot of the statue of Dionysus and the crowd somewhat stilled in reverence as they listened to the accolades bestowed on Dionysus by the poets of old. Kids ran through the market, chasing each other and tossing sticks. Mostly, people drank and acted like they'd never had a day of pleasure before, even though the festival was a yearly occurrence.

Alexios slipped onto a side street near the temple that spoked out from the courtyard, his tunic catching on a bush as he brushed by. He tugged it loose and hurried into the smaller alley at his right. The burning smell of the public urinals seized his lungs. Coughing, he made his way past the portable basins set out to capture waste during the festival. Athens prided itself on providing a fine place to piss.

"Ugh," Mattan said, holding his nose. "We can't talk here."

Alexios chuckled at the hidden irony. "Down here," he pointed, "by the water."

A tall, marble fountain towered at the end of the narrow street, flanked by flat, stone benches and tables. A few women gathered, dipping hand-painted terra-cotta pots into the basin around the fountain, then carting away the heavy jugs of fresh water, no doubt to hydrate their drunken husbands or to wash the day's celebrations away. The fountain was spring-fed and refilled itself automatically, with the excess draining into a larger pool below. No doubt about it, Athens birthed the finest engineers in the world.

Where else could a person get fresh water to drink and also relieve themselves?

He sat on a low bench near the fountain and Mattan dropped down beside him, sprawling and folding his arms over his chest. Considering the size of the crowd in the courtyard, Alexios was surprised that the fountain lay almost deserted. The women were gone and he and Mattan were the only people nearby, save an older woman hobbling toward them.

Birds landed on the upper fountain, flapping and vying for position on the edge of the basin. A large, white dove, the bird of Aphrodite, landed and the other, lesser birds scattered. The dove looked at Alexios, blinked its golden eyes then craned its neck and dipped an orange beak in the cool water.

Was it one of the doves released by the *archon?*

"Tell me. Any progress?" Mattan fiddled with his filthy tunic. "You know how impatient the playwright gets."

"I only found out my task two days ago," Alexios replied. "It'll take time." He watched the older woman approach the splashing fountain, dip her pot in, and heave it up to her shoulder. She stumbled a bit under the weight then padded back the way she'd come.

"Did you see him?"

"Who?" Alexios stared at the white bird preening on the marble. Such a lovely creature.

"Kallistos."

"I saw him."

The dove startled and took flight and he watched it soar over the street, one wing dipped low, then disappear.

"We only have a few days—could be as few as two if he gets the first draw. First position would be best, since those plays are oft forgotten by the third day. But we can't count on him drawing that lot. We have to be prepared for anything."

Alexios studied the man a moment, then leaned forward and whispered, "I'll get to Kallistos. One way or another, his plays will fail. Sophocles needn't worry."

"For your sake, I hope you're right."

"I'll take care of it. Then he'll give me a part in a play." Alexios wrapped the ivy tighter around his neck and tugged the ends.

"Maybe," Mattan said.

"He's afraid of losing." The fountain's flowing water splashed against the side of the basin in a spiral. "Maybe he should focus on his writing and stop worrying about others. It's not as if he's a bad writer."

"I agree. Seems a waste of resources to sabotage the other plays. He could be partying with the young women. Much more fun."

"I really don't care what he does. I want to be on stage, and this is a sure way to gain consideration."

"You want the money. And the fame." Mattan cleared his throat. "What price are you willing to pay?"

"The money's secondary." Alexios pushed his hair behind his ears. "I want to be a great actor. Who better to direct me than Sophocles?" He looked at Mattan, wondering if he ever wanted to be more than a stagehand. Did he understand what was at stake?

Mattan shook his head. "Lofty goal for a shepherd. And not a likely outcome. Unless performing on a hillside for the sheep is your idea of a great play."

"Close your mouth, Mattan. I'll be on stage. It's a matter of time, only." Annoyance seized Alexios' stomach and he clenched his teeth to focus on it passing. He'd spent too many nights on a cold, dark hillside under the stars dreaming of being an actor to give up now. He'd make it, no matter what it took. Taking down Kallistos was only the beginning. He'd prove his loyalty to Sophocles and once he had a chance on the big stage, he'd show everyone.

"Sheep boy. You've about as much chance of being a famous actor as I do." Mattan stood and put his hands on his hips. "You'll end up doing all your acting in the beds of the wealthy. Mark my words, that's all Sophocles is after."

"Don't speak to me that way."

"Remember this—Sophocles is using you. Like he has used fifty young men before you. And when he calls you to turn down his blankets, you'll be there. Just like the others."

Alexios boiled. Mattan was such a bastard. "I'll tend myself. You needn't worry about whose blankets I'm under."

"I'm not worried. You'll either succeed or you won't. But I suggest you don't screw this up. Otherwise, you'll wish that shepherding was an option."

"Get out of my sight."

Mattan strode off, palming the ass of a young girl who'd stepped up to the fountain to get water. She skittered away, dropping her pot into the pool. Mattan turned and winked at Alexios. "That's how you do it," he called. "Acting lesson number one."

Alexios shook his head. What a barbarian. Finessing Kallistos would take more than a pat on the ass or asking him to share a blanket. No, the playwright would need something much more complex and imaginative.

TWO

*O*il lamps flickered at the corners of the city square and the dense smoke they created filled the air with a hazy veil. The moon wavered behind the smoke—lighting the areas the lamps couldn't reach. Platters of baked fish, dried figs, and fresh bread covered the tables of the street vendors. Fruit spilled from baskets lining the path, and wine filled large tubs on nearly every corner.

Kallistos held his red terra-cotta *kylix* up and drank. The cup had a painting of Poseidon and a water horse on the inside…a perfect symbol for the upcoming plays. The wine sloshed over the painting like a stormy sea, Poseidon riding the wave of bubbles, spear held high. The night was early, but he couldn't wait to retire and go over his plays in his mind once again. The parties were of no interest to him and Stephanos could handle the publicity.

"How's the wine?" Stephanos edged closer, shoulder to shoulder.

The dancers flung themselves upon one other as the music fluted in higher octaves. They danced with long sheets of fabric, billowing the material about their bodies as they moved to the frenetic music. Around them, acrobats flipped and spun, tossing each other like fishing nets.

Kallistos nodded, his gaze fixed on the performers. "Passable. I'm looking forward to the Chian wine you promised me."

"I have a dozen *amphoras* at my house waiting for the celebration of your win. I have to warn you; one drink and you won't return to the muscat grape."

"Perhaps. I favor sweet wine, even if it's fare for commoners."

Stephanos thumped him on the back. "Well, don't be late getting to my house. The morning sun will come earlier than you think. And it will bring us the news."

"The order of performances." Kallistos turned up his cup and finished off the wine. "Pray I am last on the list!"

"And the old grouch is first."

"May the gods hear our wishes." He backed away from a man who danced too close, flailing in rapture to the music. "Any information about the other plays?"

The crowd laughed in unison as one of the acrobats tossed another into a pile of hay.

"Rumor is that Sophocles is doing King Minos." Stephanos leaned closer.

"The minotaur? That should be an interesting costume." He paused. He'd not considered a play about the wayward bull, and his mind took him off into thought. The frantic display of cloth in front of him made him think of the angry bull and its lost mate.

"And Daedalus." Stephanos raised his voice above the noise.

"Huh?"

"Daedalus," Stephanos repeated.

Kallistos shook his head. "Daedalus has been done so many times. What could he bring to that story that is new?"

"I don't know but with it being Sophocles, who knows? Best bet? Worry about your own plays and the workings of that horse," Stephanos said. "I'll find out as much as I can about the other plays tonight. I'll tell you anything I find out."

"Good." Kallistos nodded. "And the third participant? Any news on what he might perform?"

"The abduction of Persephone, if accounts are correct."

"How exciting."

"How tragic."

"The audience loves a good tragedy."

"They do. I hope your Achilles dies well."

"He must."

"Make them weep!"

Two giggling girls pushed another girl forward toward Kallistos. She wobbled as she walked the remaining few steps toward him, her hair undone from its tiered pile of curls. It trailed about her shoulders like a damp mane of sea grass. "Will you dance?" she warbled.

Kallistos looked to Stephanos, stricken, and took a step back. His palms dampened, and his stomach burned. Dancing? With a girl? A stranger? Surely Stephanos didn't expect him to mingle so much. Touching someone, a girl even, that he didn't know… that was unacceptable.

Stephanos must have sensed his unease.

"Go away, you drunken birds. Kallistos doesn't have time to dance tonight. Cheer his plays and maybe he'll grant you a favor at the winner's celebration." He shooed the girls with his hands.

The fact they even approached him meant they were most assuredly drunk. They'd likely not remember with the morning light.

Kallistos smiled and cast his eyes down. The girls twittered and pulled the drunken one away, laughing and stumbling. Within a moment, they were lost in the throng of revelers. He was forgotten, as he wished.

The grape held magical powers.

"Thank you." Kallistos took a deep breath. "I think she must have been quite young. And quite drunk."

"I know your heart lies elsewhere, and with the stronger sex at that. But these few days, during the festival, you belong to me. The last thing you need is a distraction from your plays."

An acrobat pushed past, balancing colorful bowls on his head and dancing as he contorted his arms. He nodded toward Kallistos as he passed and for a moment, the bowls teetered on his head. He righted them and kept moving.

"I have no need of companionship," Kallistos said.

"Well, pay heed. Everyone wants to spend time with the fair-haired, green-eyed actor. It's an opportunity to influence people and get them to support your art. As long as your plays are well received, you'll continue to be sought out."

"I don't want to be sought out like some different butterfly to collect."

Stephanos harrumphed. "One day, you won't want to be lonely. When that time comes, you'll find your love. For now, focus on your fame."

Kallistos sighed. "No more nonsense about love and companionship. I want to know my position in the lineup now. The sun can't return soon enough."

"Go on to my home and rest, letting go of all thoughts except your performance. My servants will attend you and make sure you are awakened in time to go to the theater. I'll campaign for you tonight."

"Thank you. I'm in agreement." He yawned. "A cup of wine to drink on the way, and I'll sleep well. When we wake, we'll meet our fate. May it be a reward."

He raised his empty cup in salute. A gang of young men jostled him as they bumped through the crowd like a pack of drunken wolves. One of the men whistled at him, before the others dragged the gawker away.

Stephanos patted him on the back. "You'd best be going, before you have more than your share of boyfriends. I'll find your other actors and see what they're doing. Hopefully not spoiling the surprise."

"I told them to keep quiet, so I don't think they will spoil the surprise. I do worry a little about Bion. He is most likely to drink and talk."

"I'll find him. You rest."

Kallistos headed toward the wine vendor. Thankfully, the city paid for all the wine and everyone could drink as much as they wished, though tonight, he'd almost had enough.

By the gods, the man was gorgeous.

Alexios watched Kallistos fill his wine cup. Had no one else seen his beauty? Kallistos stood alone, cup to his lips.

In the lamplight, his body gleamed like spun gold and his light hair sparkled as if it were wet with morning dew. His simple tunic clung to him, its belt cinching his narrow waist. Spending time with the beautiful one would be a pleasure, not a chore. And he wouldn't have to work at finding the pleasures that body had to offer, given the chance.

A large man stepped in front of him, blocking his sight and Alexios moved so he could keep his view. It was almost absurd that work could be so pleasurable. He could watch Kallistos all day, though he needed to approach the beautiful one soon. For the moment, he'd watch, though Kallistos was more than aloof in his posture. Too beautiful to be so reserved.

He followed Kallistos onto the darker streets away from the square where the noise lessened, and the crowd thinned. In the distance, fires twinkled on the Acropolis like tiny sparks of birthing stars, fizzing and bursting in the darkness. The Parthenon, though it had only stood for a handful of time, crowned the Acropolis like a golden diadem, with spears of light radiating from behind its columns and streaking into the evening. Athena smiled down from her position of guardian, high above the city.

Alexios sped to get closer to Kallistos, having briefly forgotten his plan. The city did that. Its magnificence wasn't rivaled, and he was quite sure that Athens was magical. The land where he tended sheep was charming with its rusticity—but Athens held an unparalleled enchantment. To live in the city, attend its parties, and act on its stages would be a life's dream.

He caught up to Kallistos and walked a few paces behind. Even from this angle, the man was gorgeous. People passed him by, casting glances at the fair-haired man. If Alexios was going to make an introduction, it was time.

"Kallistos. Wait." His voice sounded entirely not his own, but like a voice from the depths of the soothsayer's cave.

Kallistos stopped. "Who calls my name?"

"An admirer."

"I've no time for admirers. Step into the lamplight."

Alexios' stomach trembled at the tenor of Kallistos's voice. He stepped out of the shadows into the half light of the street.

"What do you want?" Kallistos asked. He held his wine cup steady and looked away. "I'm too tired to entertain but you are welcome to come see my plays in the *theatron*."

The way Kallistos dipped his head in slight embarrassment, shrugging his shoulders as he spoke, warmed Alexios from the inside out. "Begging your forgiveness," he said, "but I wanted to talk to the playwright Kallistos and maybe share wine. It would be an honor."

Kallistos paused for a moment before speaking, digging his sandal toe against the dirt road. Would he yell or rebuff the intrusion? He brought his wine to his lips, tipping the cup high. The muscles in his neck clenched as the wine went down his throat.

Alexios tensed. Maybe this wasn't going to be as easy as he thought.

"You have me at a disadvantage," Kallistos said, lowering the empty cup. "You know my name, but you've not told me yours."

He moved closer. "I'm Alexios."

"Alexios," Kallistos repeated.

His name rolled off Kallistos's tongue like a silken promise.

"I've come to Athens for the festival and I heard about your plays." The words stumbled out, and Alexios shifted. Since when did a man make him quiver without a touch?

Kallistos frowned. "What have you heard?"

"I've heard your participation in Great Dionysia will rival Sophocles."

"I can only hope for such glory."

"Your wife and children must be proud." Was his attempt to gather information too bold?

Time slowed, and he waited on the answer.

"I have no wife, nor wish to find one. My plays are my lovers." Kallistos looked up toward the moon and fiddled with his wine cup. "I have to go. But I'd like to see you again, Alexios. Perhaps we can discuss philosophy over some finer wine than this street vintage." He smiled and briefly made eye contact.

Alexios fought the shudder that racked his body. "I'd like that. It isn't every day a shepherd is offered the chance to share philosophy with a famous playwright."

"I'm not famous, but I'll count you among my fans, shepherd."

"Do so."

Kallistos met his gaze for a few moments before looking down. "Until another day, then." He turned to leave.

"Wait." Alexios grabbed his arm.

Kallistos gasped, his eyes wide in the soft moonlight. "Will you harm me, shepherd?"

Alexios trailed his hand down Kallistos's bare arm, feeling the soft blond hairs under his fingertips. He gulped as heat shot straight to his groin. "Never will I harm you. May the gods, if they exist, shine favor on you in the *theatron*."

Kallistos shivered and Alexios' stomach tightened.

"And may Dionysus himself guide your travels tonight," Kallistos said. He lingered for a moment, then slipped out of Alexios's grasp and walked on.

Alexios stood on the darkened street, his mind ablaze. His breath caught at the thought of what might have happened if he had pulled Kallistos closer into an embrace. Had the beautiful one been offering himself? He shook his head. Surely, he was not. He was only being polite.

A stiff wind whipped through the street and Alexios held his fluttering tunic against his body, snapping from the reverie that had overtaken him.

Focus. He hadn't been hired to befriend Kallistos or take him as a lover. His one goal was to destroy Kallistos's chances of winning the festival.

KALLISTOS TAPPED the cup against his hand as he walked. His legs shook, and it wasn't from the base wine he'd consumed in gulps. The same man he had seen during the procession—the same dark hair, and deep, dark eyes—had found him on the streets of

Athens. It couldn't be a coincidence. But why would the man seek him out?

Perhaps Athena had sent him as a muse. Or maybe even Dionysus was smiling favors upon the playwrights. Kallistos's chest buzzed with the exhilaration of the dark stranger's touch on his arm. A firm grip, stroking his skin with warmth and promise.

A promise he could never fulfill.

He stumbled over a rut in the road and caught himself before falling. He was losing focus on the task ahead and it was Alexios's fault. The man held some kind of magic in his words. He had to keep his attention on the contest, not on physical pleasure. Stephanos would be enraged if he didn't.

The plays were ready. The props were at Stephanos's house, and the masks and costumes were waiting to be worn. Everything was in place.

How easily everything could be ruined.

Then again, why shouldn't he have a bit of fun now that things were ready? What was the harm? Everyone else in Athens seemed to make the most of the wine and dancing at festival. Why should he, alone, suffer with duty?

It is who I am. No man could tempt him away from his life's passion—his plays.

Besides, Alexios would never understand his shyness. Kallistos could talk to men, but his true communication had always manifested through his writing—his plays and poetry. How would he ever discuss philosophy with such a worldly man as Alexios, much less try to tempt him to do other things. Heat rushed his face at the thought and he rubbed it with his free hand.

Surely their paths would not cross again in the large city—there were so many people in Athens for the festival. The odds were against him. Or for him, depending on how it was perceived.

He stepped into the small, overgrown courtyard in front of Stephanos's house. The larger props for his play sat in the walled back garden, invisible to prying eyes—and the front of the house gave no indication that one of the Dionysian playwrights slept there. Just as well. Rest was what he needed, not more people wanting to talk to him, dance with him, have wine. He walked up the stone-lined walk, clutching the wine cup.

If he had another cupful, he wouldn't be sorry, though he might be in the morning.

A servant stood at the heavy door, and opened it when he knocked, nodding to him as he passed. The air in the house hit him like a warm, sticky breath, and the glowing lamps trailed banded shadows along the walls like long fingers.

The *archon* had been kind to him, indeed. Not every playwright was bound to such a wealthy sponsor, or one so well known. Sophocles funded his own plays—using his sponsor to manage the parties and guests. The third playwright? He didn't know what his circumstances were, but it was best not to worry at all. He'd make sure his own plays were the best they could be and that was it.

"I'm going to sleep." He handed the wine cup to the servant who'd trailed him from the front door. "See that I'm not disturbed until morning."

"May sleep find you easily and may morning find you well rested," the servant said. "Your bed is ready."

If Alexios visits my dreams, I won't rest. His groin throbbed, and he pushed the thoughts away, at least for the moment. He ducked into his room, half-hoping his dreams would be realized when Hypnos and Morpheus came to visit in the night.

"Kallistos, wait!"

"What now?" He stepped into the hallway. "Bion. You aren't out celebrating?"

"I was. Did you hear?" The man was breathless,

his mid-back length, brown hair tied with twine and his crooked nose flaring.

"Hear what?" He ran a hand through his hair and stifled a yawn. He'd had more wine than intended, and it was plying him.

Bion drew closer, his lanky frame towering over Kallistos. Wine rolled off him like heavy mist over a meadow. He was a great actor, but he surely loved his wine, sometimes too much.

"It's Sophocles."

"Is he ill?" Kallistos stepped back against the cool, plastered wall. If Sophocles couldn't compete, what would happen? Would the festival be cancelled?

"No, no." Bion waved him off. "He's as well as he ever was. That surly old man will outlive us all." He laughed and pulled the top of his tunic into place.

"Then what? What happened?"

"Sit. You aren't going to like it. It's big."

"Tell me. I'm too tired for games." Kallistos collapsed on one of the low seats in the long hallway, tossing a pillow aside. He'd worked with Bion long enough to not be shy around him, but the man's overbearing presence was often too much to deal with.

"Well," Bion said. He burped loudly. "Sophocles has a major revelation planned. One that will rival our horse, if not overshadow it. At least it seems like it will."

"Quiet." Kallistos leaned forward. "We don't want the servants overhearing and spreading rumors."

"Oh everyone already knows. Sophocles is the master of promotion—you know that. He's made sure to get the details out. I think every whore in the city is spreading the information as often as she spreads her—"

"And…what is the information?" Kallistos shifted. Frustration grew from the pit of his stomach like a viper and coiled up through his abdomen to his throat. Bion was a storyteller, but now was not the time. Sweet dreams beckoned, and the wine clouded his thoughts. News of something big from Sophocles was the last thing he wanted to hear.

Bion paused. "Word is all over Athens that he commissioned a minotaur mask—of solid gold and encrusted with gems. No minotaur ever paraded in such glory as this costume will hold. The beast will leap from the darkness under the stage and rival the sun."

"Oh." Acid filled Kallistos's mouth. How would he compete with such extravagance? Gold and gems? His props were wood with a little paint. Nothing fancy at all.

"The judges are likely to be so amazed by the mask that they won't even pay attention to the play. He'll win on the mask alone." Bion lay back on the seat. "At least that is the rumor."

"Then we have to be better." Kallistos stood.

"How? Our horse is large, but it isn't made of gold! And I hear the minotaur's robe will be of finest China silk, brought over the mountains and through snowy passes." Bion burped again then wiped his mouth.

Oh gods. This was bad.

Kallistos paced. His head pounded and he tried to exhale and release the stress knotting him up from his toes to the top of his head. How would he compete? It was true that the appearance of such magnificent props could swing the whole competition to Sophocles's favor. But surely there was something he could do.

My plays are better, by the gods.

"What are we going to do? I know we expect he'll win regardless, but this feels like a certainty. I'd hoped we at least stood a chance." Bion yawned, stretching his hands above his head then dropping them into his lap.

Kallistos frowned. "Sophocles is full of tricks, but no one has seen the likes of a horse the size of ours.

It'll make the judges gasp. And our acting will be unparalleled. We still have a chance to win."

"Let's hope."

"Have faith, Bion. Our plays are solid, with many surprises. We may not have Sophocles's fame or wealth, but we won't be ashamed of what we do. We'll do our best and see what the judges rule."

Bion stretched out on the low couch and fingered the ropes tying the fabric to the frame. "I hope you're right. I'd like nothing better than to best the old man."

"On that, we agree."

THREE

Kallistos stood at the top of the hill where the tall grass bowed to the wind. Over his shoulder, the Acropolis loomed, as if the gods watched the play below in the *theatron*. Wooden bleachers, hewn from logs and dragged by horseback to Athens, already mostly filled to capacity, fanned out below him. The flat, brown semicircle of the stage perched at the bottom of the hill like half a coin, awaiting the drama to be unveiled. The crowd murmured and buzzed like a swarm of insects and the scent of wine permeated the air.

Will my horse be impressive from high in the stands, or will it look like a pony? Certainly, a golden mask will gleam and sparkle like a thousand suns.

The *skene*, with its newly added wings and

porches, stood tall enough to conceal the horse until it rolled out from around the back to make its entrance. The newer *skene* held rooms for changing, props, and resting places for the actors and was one of the best equipped anywhere.

It was an honor to be performing in the great *theatron* of Athens. Thankfully, the building additions would mask the horse until time—the trick would be delivering the horse on the night before the plays. It would lose its excitement if people saw it beforehand.

"You ready?" Stephanos gripped Kallistos' shoulder. "Let's get down there before they introduce you."

"I'm ready."

The sacrifices to Dionysus had been made as the sun lifted over the mountains, and slaves now cleaned the bloody altar. Already, Kallistos could smell the roasting beef and lamb that would provide the day's feast. With Stephanos holding onto his shoulder, he made his way down the sloping stairs, pushing through people searching for seats. The crowd hummed with excitement and lack of sleep, and many reached out to touch his tunic as he passed. He avoided thinking about being in such a large crowd and focused on getting down the stairs.

He would know soon. After the tributes had been

offered, the order of performances would be drawn by lot and the die would be cast.

Hopefully, the fates would smile on him.

They circled around the orchestra area to the *paraskenia*. The early morning sunlight backlit the statue of Dionysus and his fennel staff and cast his long shadow across the stage and over the central altar. He had a fresh crown of laurel leaves and a trailing necklace of ivy.

"He's watching us," Kallistos murmured.

"May he smile on us through the selection process."

Kallistos nodded. "I'm going to check out our props area and make sure we have space for the weapons and masks."

"When do you plan to move them?" Stephanos wiped his brow. The early sun warmed the hillside, and not a cloud passed through the sky to obscure the day's importance.

"Bion and Diokles will bring them over this evening," Kallistos said. "It shouldn't take long. I need to make sure there's plenty of room for everything."

"What about the horse?" Stephanos whispered. "That's going to take several men to move."

"We'll move it late at night—right before my

performance, whenever that is. I'll need some of your servants' help."

"Use as many of my men as you need." Stephanos scanned the crowd gathering at the stage's edge.

"Thank you."

"Ah, there is the *archon*! I must go thank him for his graciousness. Go ahead and check your props room and I'll meet you before the selection."

Kallistos nodded and watched Stephanos move to greet the *archon*. The festival organizer would be the one overseeing the drawing of lots for position—with as much pomp as possible. That was his job. Citizens, women, and slaves alike enjoyed the festivities.

Kallistos grimaced as his stomach lurched. Thankfully, the drawing would begin soon, and he could retreat to Stephanos's house. Oddly, crowds made him ill unless he was performing in front of them.

It was a good thing Stephanos had no trouble chatting up the dignitaries and rubbing elbows with the elite. If Kallistos had to do all the promotion on his own, he'd never have submitted his plays for selection. He'd rather not participate than be forced to schmooze.

Dust rose over his sandals as he walked, and he kept his head down so that no one would call him out.

He stepped into the darkened arch that led into the

paraskenia. The building was quiet and dark except for a few oil lamps positioned along the walls, and the temperature was cooler. It was a nice respite from the sun and noisy crowd, though he could still hear a low rumbling of conversation from the bleachers above. The long corridor just inside the entrance opened into a large room for staging, then branched off to several dressing rooms and even a latrine. Near the end of the hallway were three larger rooms with fabric hanging over the doorways. Initialed clay tablets marked whose room was whose. He stepped into the room labeled "K".

The props chamber had three small openings near the ceiling and the morning light fell through them and half-lit the room in a cherry tint. A couple of cots were pushed against the far wall, and a small table with a basin sat against the side wall. No doubt *amphoras* of wine would be delivered soon and replenished throughout the next three days. There was plenty of room to store his props against the near wall, and still have space to relax and wait between plays.

Athens provided. He'd really needed a moment of quiet before the ceremonies began, but Stephanos would've scoffed. Checking out the prop storage had seemed to be a valid escape.

The crowd cheered and stomped, causing the air to vibrate. The room was not closed in enough to be a complete barrier to the noise but dampened it to a hum. The tributes from outlying towns were being made and the crowd responded enthusiastically to each offering.

In previous years, he'd seen the tributes and offerings. Piles of silver and wood, fabrics, and live animals were shown off on stage—all given by the cities Athens protected. The wealthier the city, the greater the offerings. The military was on full parade and circling the orchestra as the tributes were announced, then they'd carry everything to the Acropolis for treasury distribution. No one who'd seen the vast wealth could doubt the influence Athens had on the world. It was the greatest city and worked hard to make sure everyone knew it.

Fortune smiled on the citizens of Athens.

Kallistos moved to stand in the strip of rosy sunlight that poured in from one of the windows and imagined the cheers were for him. Soon, they would be. Or maybe he'd be jeered.

He closed his eyes and remembered being in the *theatron* many years before, when he was a child. He'd stood at the top of the hillside theater seats and watched the great general Pericles drilling his men in preparation for the tribute ceremony. One of the men spotted him spying and had shouted for Kallistos to leave, but Pericles had called him down and had him sit in the front row to watch. He'd said something that had stayed with Kallistos all the years since. "Strive, young boy, to make your mark on this stage as I do. Lead men, do not be led by them."

Kallistos stood tall. Being a playwright was not what Pericles had meant, but it was ironic all the same. He would strive. And he would succeed. He breathed the moment in deeply.

"Kallistos?" A whisper came from behind the fabric door. "Are you in there?"

"Come in." He turned to see who called.

Alexios stepped inside and Kallistos drew in a breath. The room suddenly felt much smaller. "You shouldn't be here."

You shouldn't. But everything in my being screams joy that you are near again.

"I had to see you."

"Can't talk to you right now. It's almost time to draw lots for play order. How did you get in here? Only people helping with the performances are allowed in this area."

"I snuck in through the rear door—there was no one near. I hoped you'd be inside." Alexios closed the gap between them and stood within a breath. "I had to see you, if you were here. Before the day became too busy. Before you forgot your promise."

Kallistos stepped back against the wall and Alexios followed, leaning in close but not touching. Heat radiated from him and Kallistos' stomach tensed. He was so near, the hem of his tunic surely brushed against the other man.

"What do you ask of me?"

"Meet me in front of the Parthenon after the ceremony. I'll bring lunch and we can have that talk you promised. I'll bring wine. Good stuff. We can debate the great truths." Alexios's voice wavered as he spoke.

"I…I…can't." Kallistos ducked his head, then flushed when he realized Alexios probably thought he was staring at his groin. He raised his head and met Alexios's hot stare.

"Shh." Alexios pushed close. "It's fine. You don't need to be shy. I won't hurt you, I promise."

Alexios pinned him against the cool wall and he felt the hard ridge between his thighs pressing against a similar hardness. His knees weakened, and he fought the urge to thrust against Alexios. There was no time for distractions. No matter how tempting.

Focus.

"I..." Kallistos breathed in short puffs and sweat broke out on his back and trailed down his spine.

I have to focus.

"You must meet with me. Please. I've thought about you since last night and I want to...talk."

"Why me?" Kallistos squeaked. His face flushed. The hesitation in Alexios' sentence held secrets—and promises.

As much as he wanted to give in, he had to stay focused on his plays. On beating Sophocles. Maybe after it was all over, he'd have time to get to know Alexios properly. His head swam with the weight of emotion.

"I want to learn everything about you." Alexios's voice hummed low. "I want to know what keeps you awake in the dark night and what makes your heart swell with joy. I want to know all your secrets, beautiful one. Have lunch with me. Talk. What harm could come to you?" He pushed his hips against Kallistos, never taking his gaze from him. "We all have to eat. How could it be bad to eat together?"

Kallistos groaned and closed his eyes. What harm, indeed? Any time but now, just before the City Dionysia, he would have seriously considered Alexios's offer. He'd never responded to another person this way—not so hot and so fast. Alexios, despite his forwardness, didn't scare him the same way other people did.

What was it that fueled his attraction to him? It wasn't the attention—many had tried to seduce him before, and few had succeeded in gaining his attention, much less his body. Was the thought so terrible? What could it hurt to explore the friendship of this man? His body shook with urges he hadn't felt so deeply before.

Alexios pressed his warm lips on Kallistos's and ran his tongue across his closed mouth, wetting his lips with one stroke. Kallistos quivered and his lips parted as he breathed in Alexios. Just for a moment, he savored the kiss. He was sure Alexios could feel his heart thumping—and his erection straining. He reached for him, running his hands across Alexios's broad, warm back, feeling the ridges of muscles that flexed as they held each other.

For a moment, they were alone together, and the City Dionysia retreated from his mind and all he felt was the warmth of the other man breathing in time with him. His thoughts floated away, and he held on tight.

Alexios suddenly pulled away and Kallistos jerked—feeling as if half of his body had been ripped away and cold sand poured into the emptiness. He panted, wide-eyed, at the man standing before him.

"You will come?" He was sure there was a twinkle in Alexios's eyes.

Kallistos nodded, touching his numb lips to make sure he wasn't dreaming. Refusing Alexios was impossible. Besides that, he wanted to see him again.

Kallistos scanned the crowd for Alexios, but there was little to no chance of spotting him in the throng of people. The bleachers creaked with citizens anxious to hear the order of performances and Kallistos chastised himself for not being attentive. Most of the people in the stands would attend all the performances, but many likely wanted to see the great Sophocles take the coveted third position. The last play performed held an advantage.

Everyone remembered it.

The ache in his groin had subsided, but his lips still buzzed from the disrupted kiss. Alexios had dashed off, leaving him with so many questions. Why had Alexios taken an interest in him? Had he not rebuffed him enough in the street? No, he'd asked him to meet to talk. What madness had his mind led him to? He shifted foot to foot, the hot sun beating on his back.

Though he needed to focus on the ceremony, much of his thoughts centered on meeting up with Alexios to talk and eat.

And kiss, gods willing.

The tributes had been cleared away and the sponsors, playwrights, and actors stood in a semicircle around the altar, waiting for the drawing of lots. Sophocles sat in his chair, not even bothering standing with everyone else. He didn't appear nervous at all.

Finally, the *archon*, sitting in a large, stone throne, raised his hand and the chorus of men at the base of the statue of Dionysus chanted their short prayer. The audience answered in unison. Priests, in their headdresses of laurel and wearing goat horns, danced around the statue next, placing pots of smoky incense at the god's feet.

The sun beat hot on Kallistos's back and sweat pooled beneath his robe and trailed down over his torso. The dust in the air gave a hazy aura to the *theatron*, making the crowd appear to waver and vibrate in a massive mirage. Today, the spectators were eager for information. At his performance, they'd wait to be entertained, and they'd throw things at him if they didn't like his plays. He shuddered.

Only defeat by Sophocles would be worse than the audience's vitriol.

The chorus stopped, their last note reverberating then dying off in echo along the hillside. The *archon* stood and walked toward the altar where a tall urn sat. The urn was painted with pictures of tragedies of old, and Kallistos hoped it would bring good fortune rather than bitter defeat. Inside, the numbers of the plays were cast as lots upon the ground.

The order of performance would be decided, for better or for worse.

"With the blessing of Dionysus, we will now determine which playwright will perform on each day of the festival." The crowd rumbled. "Sponsors will draw the lots and playwrights will make last preparations. Performances start with the rising sun tomorrow. Tonight, we will feast in honor of Dionysus."

The crowd stomped its feet and the thumping resonated in the amphitheater and throughout Kallistos's body. *Here we go. Not first. Not first place.* He took short, sharp breaths, and waited.

"Nikator, sponsor of Silas, you draw first," the *archon* said. The crowd stilled as Nikator approached the urn.

Stephanos shrugged and Kallistos drew in a deep breath. Worst case, Kallistos would be stuck with the first performance. He should focus on the positive and be grateful he was selected to perform at all. So many playwrights would never get the chance at all. He'd already been successful compared to most, and now he'd meet Sophocles—the test of any playwright's mettle. And later, he'd meet up to dine with Alexios. His stomach flip-flopped.

A servant held the urn high so no one could see inside. Nikator bowed to the *archon* and pulled Silas up beside him. The man stumbled and almost fell, but Nikator caught him and whispered in his ear. The crowd chanted as Nikator reached into the urn, pulled out a small, clay disk and handed it to the *archon*.

"Position one!" The archon held the clay tile in the air for everyone to see. The crowd cheered, waving colored cloths in the air and stomping the ground in unison. Nikator scowled and hugged Silas. Both men tensed, then Silas stormed away with fists clenched. No one wanted to be first.

Kallistos looked toward Sophocles. The old man sat in a chair, unmoving. Even the men around him glowed with his reflected glory. They leaned toward him like they were both trying to be in his presence and also protecting him.

How did he ever think he could defeat the legend? It didn't seem possible to overcome the myth.

"Next to draw will be Bakphos for Sophocles." The *archon* paced.

If Kallistos thought the crowd had roared before, he had only heard with one ear. The spectators jumped to their feet, screaming, stomping, and waving their arms at the mention of Sophocles. Strips of fabric fluttered over the crowd and the whole *theatron* seemed to be moving in slow motion. The throng undulated, wild and unkempt like the snakes swarming on Medusa's head, only this crowd didn't turn men to stone. No, these men were already in thrall to Sophocles.

Bakphos reached to help Sophocles stand. As the playwright rose, grasping his staff until his knuckles whitened, he waved at the crowd and the screaming and stomping frenzy grew louder. His long beard quivered, and he moved steadily toward the urn.

Lone crowd members screamed his name, but Sophocles didn't turn. He focused on the urn, his jaw set, and eyes narrowed.

"Silence!" The *archon* raised his hand. "We need to hear the number drawn. Give the great Sophocles his due respect, I beg of you." The sound carried up the *theatron* banks and the crowd gradually quieted. Everyone wanted to see Sophocles's draw.

"I will defer my draw." Bakphos bowed.

Kallistos slowed his breathing, hoping to not show his nervousness. Even if Sophocles got the coveted third position, it wasn't the worst that could happen. Silas had the unluckiest position, and Kallistos was happy that he was guaranteed day two or three for his own performance.

"As you wish." The *archon* nodded to the servant holding the urn. "Sophocles will draw his own position."

Kallistos's palms sweated, and he clasped his hands together. If Sophocles drew third position, then day two would be his. Trying to convince himself that either position was fine wasn't working. Third position was most desired. His heart thudded and his throat constricted.

The pressure of the day threatened him, and his head swam. He placed a hand on Stephanos and held on for fear of fainting.

The crowd quietened when Sophocles reached for the urn, and Kallistos swore he heard everyone's intake of breath as he waited. His own sharp breath joined the crowd's, and everyone watched as Sophocles pulled a tile from the urn and spun it in the air like a gold coin. Kallistos squeezed his eyes shut and waited.

"Second position!" the *archon* shouted. "Sophocles has drawn day two!" The crowd gasped.

Sophocles didn't have best position?

Had he heard correctly? He opened his eyes just as Stephanos tackle-hugged him, almost knocking him to the ground. He straightened his tunic and blinked in the bright sunlight. He'd won the draw. His plays would be in the prime position.

"Day three! What we hoped!" Stephanos said. "The gods favor us."

Kallistos nodded, his mouth so dry he was unable to form words. Day three! Dionysus had smiled on him for sure. Now, he was on his own to woo the people. Everything had fallen into place and now it would depend on his plays and his actors.

The crowd let out a restrained cheer as the *archon* waved them quiet. They began to file out to celebrate and feast the day away while the playwrights put the final touches on their plays.

Sophocles stared, his brows turned down in distaste. Kallistos took a breath.

"May the gods favor you." Kallistos nodded his head in deference.

Sophocles grunted. "Apparently, today they favor you."

A lone, white dove swooped over the gathered crowd and landed on the altar, cooing, and Sophocles shooed it away with a swipe of his hand.

FOUR

The wind lifted off the salty sea and rushed up the hill to the Acropolis, singing over the tiled ground in the courtyard and whispering between colorful columns and statuary. Alexios leaned against the cool wall, shadowed by the imposing Parthenon. The buildings and sculptures had all been repainted for the Dionysia and everything glistened with a new and festive façade.

People swarmed the temple entrance; men sauntered in to make offerings or sat on the ground outside to talk politics or philosophy or matters of the heart. The statue of Athena, centered on the courtyard, cast a long shadow, her bronze arm raising a piercing spear to protect the city from invasion.

Where was Kallistos? Alexios had watched the

theatron empty after the drawing of lots for performance order. His heart has soared at the thought Kallistos might have been thinking of him as he stood on the storied stage. Shouts and stomps had echoed up the hillside during the drawing, and he wondered who had taken the coveted last position. The crowd favorite was certainly Sophocles, but the other playwrights had cheers too. Athens took care of its playwrights, treating them as the best among men.

Though he hoped Sophocles had secured the last position, it was impossible to tell the outcome from where he rested in the shade. A small part of him wished that fortune had favored Kallistos, though he could never utter the words.

He picked up the basket of food he'd picked up for their lunch and headed over to the stairs near the entrance to the Parthenon. As he approached, he spotted Kallistos seated on the lower stair. He looked up and his face softened.

"You came." Alexios warmed.

"I've got a little while. Not long. There's much work to be done before my performance." He scanned the area, his gaze flitting from person to person, but never settling on one man.

Alexios held back the urge to comfort the man, to

pat his shoulder or stroke his arm. What was Kallistos afraid of?

Surely, he doesn't know of Sophocles's plan. Or my own.

No, that wasn't possible. He was timid around people, that was all. Some men, especially artists, were that way.

"I brought lunch." He held the basket up.

"That's a kindness." Kallistos gazed down the stairs toward the *theatron* below. "Many thanks. It's been a busy morning and I'll agree that I need to eat."

"Let's move to a quieter spot. It's so busy here." Alexios motioned for Kallistos to follow.

"As you wish." Kallistos stood and straightened his tunic.

Men watched the two of them from a distance, many probably wanting to approach, but holding back because Kallistos' stance was standoffish. Alexios felt that he held a rare bird or sparkling diadem that everyone wanted to see and touch, but no one dared because it might break. Whatever power Kallistos held over him, it was not unlike a song composed of notes made of emotion, with an orchestration that transcended even the home of the gods.

Alexios led Kallistos to a small patch of vibrant grass at the opposite end of the acropolis, well away from most people. Away from the *theatron*. Hopefully away from Sophocles.

Below them, Athens spread out along the hilly terrain, its stair-stepped rows of houses and buildings like small boxes waiting to be opened by an eager child, the contents joyous and strong, representing a people of will and wonder. Alexios drew in a deep breath, the sun on his brow.

"It's so beautiful up here," he said. "I don't come to Athens often, but I love to spend time up where I can overlook the city. I wish I lived here and could enjoy this daily."

The blue sea pooled out from the rocky beaches, softening the edges. In the distance, a few islands were visible, and many boats moored in the harbor. Many had come to Athens for the festival.

"I come here to write and think. Well, I didn't when they were still working on the Parthenon. It was too noisy with all the chipping and banging. But I do love it here, close to the gods."

"You are fortunate."

"Some say so. I've only lived here a short time. If I can make my fortune here as a playwright of note, I'll be able to remain."

"No better place to be, if you can afford to live here." Alexios pulled a blanket from the top of the basket. "Let's move to the shade over there." He walked a few paces to the shadowed grass near the wall.

Kallistos nodded and followed. "I'd have thought it would be more crowded here today."

"Most are down in the streets where the wine is free. Or preparing for the dinner feast."

"That's to our benefit then." Kallistos sat cross-legged on the blanket. "We can eat without interruption."

Alexios dropped onto the blanket and scooted close to Kallistos, tugging the basket close. He made sure his elbow grazed Kallistos's arm, and the man blushed and turned away. His shyness was endearing, but his kiss had revealed the playwright's hidden passion. It ran hot under his fearful façade and Alexios was intent on experiencing it again.

Sophocles wanted him to get close to the playwright and that's what he was doing. Enjoying it was a bonus.

"I've brought bread, olives, and cheese." Alexios spread the mini feast in front of them on a smaller piece of fabric.

"It looks delicious. Thank you for gathering it."

"Oh. I also have wine, of course." He pulled a small wax-sealed decanter from the basket and set it on the blanket. "Probably not the best quality, but it was all I could easily find in such a small amount."

"It's perfect." Kallistos tapped his fingers on his knee. He stared out into the distance.

Alexios took in his profile. The soft curve of his chin and the strong cheekbones gave Kallistos the look of an aristocrat. With his light hair and eyes, his striking good looks stood out as different, but special. Did he have a parent with light hair, or was his coloring a special gift from the gods? Alexios set out two small cups then took the wine from the basket.

The heat wasn't the only thing adding to his thirst.

"Thank you for meeting me. I was afraid you wouldn't come." Alexios pulled at the wax on the wine decanter. "I know you're busy with preparing your performance."

"There's a lot left to do." A small flock of peeping birds landed on the ground beside them and Kallistos shooed them away. They rose into the sky like a long, knotted string. "But I have time for lunch."

Alexios poured the wine then plugged the decanter with the wax. He raised the glass to Kallistos. "I've been looking forward to spending some time with you."

Kallistos blushed again, rosiness creeping up his neck and over his cheeks in a wave. He picked up his cup and sipped the wine, not making eye contact. His pale skin flushed the same way it must from arousal. "Thank you. I wanted to see you again as well. Before the Dionysia became too busy."

Alexios shifted as his own body responded to his mental image of Kallistos. Getting to know him was either going to be very easy, or very difficult. Or both. Sophocles wanted to know about Kallistos's plays, and that meant getting closer to him. Maybe kissing him again. Who was he kidding? Sophocles had no expectation of kisses, only information. The kisses were purely for Alexios. He drank a gulp of the warm wine and savored its burn.

"Which performance position did you get?" he continued. "I couldn't hear."

Kallistos turned to him and his wide smile could have lit the city from sea to mountains. "Third. Can you believe it?"

"That's fantastic. That's the best spot to be in, or so everyone says." And it was. Alexios filled with happiness at the thought of Kallistos having a shot at doing well in the competition. Why he didn't favor the old man having the desired position surprised him, but the joy on Kallistos's face was contagious, and so pure. The beautiful one deserved the spot.

"Thank you. It was quite the surprise."

"The gods favored you." Alexios set his cup down. "You must be thrilled."

"I am." Kallistos sipped his wine. "I'm not sure I completely believe it yet. I assumed Sophocles would enjoy the third spot, as usual."

"He will be fine. What position did he draw?" Alexios hoped not first, as that would mean the man would be in a terrible mood when he saw him next. Sophocles wasn't tolerant of things not going his way.

"He will perform on the second day. Silas will be first."

"It will be a festival to remember." Alexios brushed the hem of his tunic. "And what plays will you perform?"

As quickly as the sun lit the sky of Kallistos's face, a thundercloud rolled over and shielded his emotion, burying it in a mire of emotion. "I can't say." His body tensed and he stopped fidgeting. "My patron wishes it to be kept a secret until it is performed."

"Oh. I'm sorry. I didn't mean to pry." Alexios picked up a piece of bread and stuffed it into his mouth. Did Kallistos realize how his emotions played across his face? There was more to it than merely keeping a secret. What had his mentor told him?

Something was going on, and he needed to find out if Sophocles was to win.

"Don't worry about it. You didn't know." Kallistos picked at the bread, popping crumbs in his mouth. "I'm uncomfortable talking much about my plays as I've had such hurdles to overcome with Sophocles competing and all."

What he said was true. Sophocles almost always won. One way or another, he'd find a way to manipulate things so that he did win. Like he was doing at the very moment. He had orchestrated things leading up to the conversation with Kallistos. All part of an overall plan to win again. Alexios scowled. The old man made him feel like goat dung.

He could have told Sophocles "no", but who would do that? Ever? Pissing off Sophocles was a sure way to ruin any future someone had in theater. Sophocles held too much power, and if he thought Alexios wasn't doing all he could to help him win? He'd see to it that herding sheep for the rest of his life was the closet Alexios would ever get to the stage.

"What's wrong?" Kallistos placed his hand on Alexios's arm. Warmth raced through him, and Alexios looked up and took in the purity and kindness on Kallistos's face. He peered into green eyes that mirrored the sea before a storm, swirling and surging.

I'd never have a real chance with him. He could never love a shepherd.

"Nothing." Alexios pulled his arm away and shoved more bread into his mouth. "Nothing is wrong."

BEADS OF SWEAT covered Alexios's olive skin, and his face shimmered. Kallistos fought the urge to push away the damp curl that stuck to his sculpted neck right where his pulse throbbed. If he touched him like that once, he wouldn't stop. Passion burned in his abdomen and he took a deep breath to diffuse its effects.

Though many Athenians showed their lust and affection out in the open, it wasn't something that appealed to him. Not that he had many relationships but making a scene in public wasn't what he wanted. And not that he was really lusting over Alexios. Was he?

He scanned the sandy tiles that paved the Acropolis. Wildflowers poked through the breaks in the stones and grassy patches dotted the area, yet only a few people milled around the Parthenon. Most people must be enjoying the free wine in the streets below, as

Alexios had said.

He adjusted himself through the folds of his robe then picked up a piece of soft cheese and pulled it apart. Flushing, he peeked at Alexios, his mouth suddenly dry. Did he notice the long strip of cheese and the way it separated from itself slowly peeling away yet clinging?

Alexios gave him a wicked look, his eyes flashing with lust, then opened his mouth. His hand trembling, Kallistos fed the strip of cheese into Alexios's wet mouth, bit by bit. Alexios closed his eyes and moaned softly, pulling his lips along the soft cheese then brushing against Kallistos's fingers.

Sweat broke out along his lip and his abdomen clenched with heat. No mistaking his arousal now, and he shook with need. He leaned closer, pushing the cheese farther and watching Alexios' soft lips envelope the end, then plant a soft kiss on his fingertips.

"That's good cheese." Alexios winked.

Kallistos nodded, his mouth parched. He reached for the wine and took several gulps, trying to chase away the image of Alexios's lips closing around the long, thin piece of cheese.

They ate in silence. Kallistos sucked a salty olive. He'd never been so smitten, so hard and so fast, by anyone. Both men and women threw themselves at him all the time. He was used to the attention his unusual looks brought.

Alexios ate quietly, and Kallistos silently thanked him for not pushing for more, though he would have bent to kiss him in a moment if asked.

Kallistos had rarely given in to temptations, as he'd always imagined a relationship was more than just a physical need. Alexios was different. He wanted the man badly—yes, it felt physical on the most basic level, but there was something else there too. Whatever it was lingered in the air between them and made the physical desire even stronger. One thing was absolute; he'd gladly give in to a physical release just to get Alexios off his mind if the festival weren't going on.

And if he weren't facing Sophocles, the greatest playwright in history.

The sun angled midway in the sky and the food was gone, eaten away in a nervous haze. Alexios lay back on the blanket, his arms folded behind his head and his eyes closed. Kallistos took the opportunity to really take in his muscular form. Alexios's unblemished olive skin and long, dark hair nearly glowed with youth and health. His tunic, loose and thin, barely concealed the form underneath.

Kallistos stifled the strong urge to touch what lay

hidden beneath the fabric folds. Surely, the curls on Alexios's head mimicked the soft curls between his legs. He swallowed hard. Need burned in his belly—low and warm. The need had begun when he first saw Alexios in the crowd at the parade and had grown stronger with each moment with him. Now, there was only one way to push the need back and find release. He would write a play about this magnificent man and his passions.

Satisfied he'd found an outlet, Kallistos watched the rise and fall of Alexios's breathing rhythm. His own breathing mirrored it and for a quiet moment, he was one with the man beside him.

"What do you think happens after you die?" Alexios asked, opening his eyes.

"I don't know." The words came out as a whisper. Thankful for a distraction, Kallistos drew his knees up and wrapped his arms around them. "I suppose we cross the river, as we are told." He shifted to hide his erection, but Alexios didn't seem to notice.

"Maybe." Alexios's gaze bore into him, the brown depths melting as he made contact then looked away.

"I guess we might go to Elysia. But that's a long-shot for those of us who are normal men."

A cluster of white birds rose up at once from the field beside them and Kallistos watched them spring into the sky on the back of the winds. Heaven seemed like a million miles away and yet at his fingertips.

"Why?" Alexios moved to lean against Kallistos and put his arm around his waist.

Kallistos stiffened but didn't move away, and Alexios rested his head, his dark curls brushing softly against Kallistos' shoulder. He smelled of woody incense and salty sweat and Kallistos breathed in the closeness. The thought of an embrace felt so right, so perfect, but he held back. He wasn't sure what Alexios wanted and he didn't want to ruin the contact they already had.

"Why is it a longshot?" Kallistos was sure his voice came out an octave higher.

"Why do you think those are our only options?" Alexios whispered. "I mean, how do you know those are our options? And how do you know that Hades even exists except in the minds of men?"

"That is what we are told." Kallistos's knees quivered. Was it from the sacrilege of the conversation or the closeness to Alexios?

"Exactly." Alexios raised his head and peered into his eyes. "It's what we're told. By other men."

"By the gods," Kallistos whispered. "It's why we have these temples. To make amends for all the stupid things human do."

Alexios placed his hand on Kallistos's exposed knee. "Has a god appeared to you and told you that you will either traverse the river Styx or romp in the Elysian Fields after your death?"

Kallistos looked around to see if anyone was listening. "Not so loud, we'll be overheard."

Alexios pulled his hand away. "You're afraid to question."

"No, a god has never directly spoken to me." Kallistos lowered his voice. "But they say that the gods speak to many. Perhaps I'm not worthy. Have they spoken to you?"

"No, nor do I think they ever will." Alexios took his hand, locking their fingers together, one-by-one. "But I do know this. You are worthy of your own beliefs. Not bound by what other men have told you. Let your mind fly free and you'll live fully."

"What is it you believe?" Kallistos squeezed Alexios's hand. The heat pooling in his lower belly had moved to his head and the world shifted and swayed under the fire of need. Everything about Alexios felt dangerous. His words, his looks, his body. All tempting him to give in.

"I believe that every man has the right to his own thoughts. His right to follow his own wishes and desires and not be subject to what other men compel."

Alexios raised Kallistos's hand to his lips and kissed it. "I'm not sure if there is an afterlife. Maybe this existence is all we have. We shouldn't squander it."

"You don't believe in the gods?" Kallistos trembled.

Alexios shrugged. "I don't know if they exist or are mere fabrications to control us. I just know, in my deepest self, that a man should follow his own mind."

"No matter what?"

"No matter what." Alexios's gaze lifted and drilled deep inside him, causing him to quake with the hum of connection.

If this connection wasn't proof of the gods, what was?

"And what if a man's desires and wishes hurt another man? Is that okay in this world without gods?" Kallistos fumbled with the words.

Alexios slipped his hand out of Kallistos's and gazed across the acropolis. "No. Of course not. We should live as we wish others to live. Never hurting another intentionally, but always helping."

Kallistos sighed, every fiber of his being thrumming with a need he couldn't have described with a thousand acts, a thousand characters, a thousand plays. He closed his eyes and leaned forward, gasping when Alexios captured his mouth with his own. They held motionless, then Alexios held Kallistos's head and kissed him deeply.

ALEXIOS HURRIED TO THE *AGORA*, Kallistos's kisses still burning his lips. They had talked until they both grew tired and then held each other and talked some more. Kallistos had to finalize props, and Alexios needed to meet Mattan, though he'd have given anything to spend more time with Kallistos instead.

The kisses were close to leading too far to turn back. Kallistos was maddeningly desirable, and yet something about him spoke of an eternity of desire. Continuing the lovemaking would only lead to both of them getting hurt—Alexios knew it and yet wished for anything but that.

As much as he needed to fulfill his commitment to Sophocles, he didn't want to hurt Kallistos. His beautiful one was exceptional in every way, and something had stirred inside Alexios' shielded heart when their lips met. Kissing him had been too pure to sully with wanton lust, though Alexios didn't know how he'd refrained from seducing the sweet man in his arms.

The sun slanted at its lowest point and cast long

shadows across the stone pavement. A few stars were already pricking the dark area of the sky.

Mattan was somewhere in the market, and Alexios headed to the spot where they'd planned to meet.

The open market pulsed with activity of the day's celebration and the scent of wine permeated the air. Dancers, musicians, and vendors clamored for space and Alexios pushed through to the area near the fountain. Not as many people gathered there and he'd be able to sit and wait.

Mattan was already there on one of the stone benches, a plump woman on his lap, his hand inside her *chiton*. She giggled and bounced on his lap as he spoke quietly to her.

"Mattan!" Alexios shook his head. The man was a pig.

Mattan pulled his hand free and wrapped his arms around the woman's waist. She threw her head back and laughed. He pulled her close as she tried to break free, arms flailing. She shoved against his chest and he let her go. She tumbled to the ground then stood up, holding on to the bench.

Alexios smirked. Wine flowed heavily during the festival, so it was no wonder things got out of control. Mattan stood, his attention no longer on the woman.

She scurried off, weaving and bobbing. No doubt she'd be on another man's lap before the night ended.

"Let's go," Alexios said. "It's too loud to talk here."

Mattan grunted and followed. "Let's get this done and over. I want to celebrate."

"Looks like you already have been."

Alexios led Mattan to the edge of the *agora* where they could find a bit of refuge from the noise. He sat on the ground and leaned against the wall of a large market building. Mattan joined him with a sigh and Alexios wondered if he would be able to get back up or if he would fall into a drunken sleep and spend the night on the street. Not that it mattered. Mattan wasn't his friend.

"What did you find out?" Mattan squinted, clearly drunk. Even in the dark shadow of the building, Alexios could see the intensity in his eyes. He might tell Sophocles that Alexios wasn't getting info.

A chill shot through him. "I'm trying."

"Trying isn't enough. What have you gotten out of him? What plays is he doing?"

"I've not gotten much of anything yet. He wouldn't tell me the plays or if he's written something completely new. Give me another day. I'll know more."

The scent of baking bread wafted by, no doubt in preparation for the next day's revelry. Incense burned in the temple, its smoky fragrance mingled with the heady wine in the street. The city showed little signs of slowing down for the evening. If anything, the party was getting wilder.

Mattan leaned close. "We don't have much time."

"I know. I had lunch with him, but he wouldn't tell me which plays."

Mattan thumped his fist on his knee. "We need to know. I heard one was about Helen of Troy."

"Where did you hear that? He hasn't spoken of anything specific." Alexios looked out over the distant, dancing crowd. People laughed and sang and drank.

The City Dionysia was a time for everyone to enjoy themselves, even women, children, and slaves. Prisoners, freed from their chains for a few days, savored the chance for free wine and sex. If an army wanted to attack, now would be the time.

"Word travels. Are you sure he didn't say anything of use?" Mattan burped and patted his stomach.

"He's afraid of Sophocles."

"He should be. The minotaur will be the greatest thing ever seen on stage. He'll bleed red stones and gallop on ivory shoes. His golden face will command the crowd to swoon in lust and terror."

Alexios nodded. "Sounds like what Sophocles would say." The minotaur would be spectacular. There was no doubt. So why did Sophocles fear the young playwright?

"He's the writer, not me." Mattan leaned in close and his wine-laced breath soured the air. "But we need to know the plays Kallistos is performing. We need to do more than break a few masks for this playwright. He's talented and a surprise could upset the balance."

"As soon as Kallistos trusts me, he'll tell me what we need to know." Dread coiled in his stomach and he longed to run from Mattan. From Sophocles.

From the beautiful one.

"See that he does trust you. Soon. Sophocles won't be happy if you don't take care of this." Mattan struggled to get to his feet. "I'll be watching. But right now, I need more wine. And maybe a nice, soft woman and some sleep." He stumbled off toward the city center.

Alexios held his head in his hands, struggling against the pounding in his skull. Why had he agreed to help Sophocles? To hurt someone for gain was wrong. Always. He believed everything he told

Kallistos. Gods or not, this was wrong. And to hurt someone so kind and so…perfect. The desire to be an actor blazed in his soul and this was his chance. Maybe the only chance he'd ever get.

What would he sacrifice to achieve it? Who would he sacrifice?

A rustling drew his attention farther down the building's side and he turned. A woman lay on the ground with a large man on top of her. She moaned softly as he pushed into her. Although they hadn't made much noise, as their passion rose, the man grunted, and the woman wrapped her legs around him and held him to her.

Transfixed, Alexios watched until the end, imagining he was the man and Kallistos lay under him. His groin surged. Another time and another place, he would have already tried to get Kallistos to lay with him. Men rarely turned him down.

The man groaned with his release and then kissed the woman, whispering promises to her on the night air. A pang of loneliness and desire shot through Alexios like a hot coal.

Kallistos would be special, different, not like the others. Everything about him felt so true and so real. Alexios frowned. He pushed down his passion and stood, intent on escaping before the couple saw him but they were already up and heading his way.

"The festival is good to men," the man said as they passed. Alexios nodded. The man's partner giggled and buried her head against his shoulder.

Alexios brushed off his clothing and rubbed his temples. Why had love always eluded him? Every time he got close, another obstacle appeared and crushed his chances. He'd had a lot of time to think about love and its various forms while tending sheep. Life was nothing without someone to share it with, and too soon life was over, and it was too late. Right?

His shoulders drooped. What about his career? Was there no way to have both?

He was a fool to think he had a real chance with the beautiful one. Kallistos would never love him once he found out about Sophocles.

Alexios didn't deserve Kallistos. Not now, not ever.

FIVE

Kallistos wiped the sweat from his forehead with the edge of his wrap. The *theatron* vibrated with noise as people stomped their appreciation for Silas's play. The first day of performances always drew a more somber crowd, usually sick from the excesses of the feast the previous night. But so far, no one had thrown things at the stage.

Kallistos sat in a chair of honor, alongside the benefactors, actors, and other playwrights. Being so close to the stage, he could analyze exactly what Silas was doing. Things had pretty much gone well, except for a few mishaps with his masks.

Silas had announced his final play, and it was about to begin. The crowd hushed, basking in the bright sunshine.

The play was *Persephone*, one of the greatest

tragedies of all time. How would Silas handle the story? How would he portray the maiden?

Kallistos leaned on his elbow and waited. Memories of Alexios's kisses the day before filled his mind and he had a difficult time focusing on the play in front of him. Alexios had stirred more than his passion. His talk about the gods had kept Kallistos awake long into the night.

Maybe the underworld truly was just a myth based on evil and pomegranate seeds? Alexios's words filled him with sacrilege yet pushed him to think. Had all the years been filled with a faith that wasn't warranted? Did gods really steer mortals through their lives, or were they answers made up to fill the void of answerless questions?

Alexios's beliefs were convincing. And yet, the gods had always seemed to smile on Kallistos. What was he to think?

Stephanos leaned close. "So far, your plays have the edge. I have no worries."

"We still have Sophocles." Kallistos sighed. He wanted to care about the plays and enjoy the moment, but what he really desired was to be with Alexios.

"We do. Let's hope that the crowd doesn't cry for Persephone."

Kallistos nodded.

An actor paraded onto stage, dressed as Persephone. The mask was gorgeous, topped by what appeared to be real hair. The actor carried a large basket overflowing with flowers and pretended to pick more as he moved over the "garden" that was the stage floor. Suddenly, a slender and unusually tall actor leapt from behind the center stage altar. His mask covered his face and continued down over his chest. Grotesque on one side, and beautifully painted on the other—this was Hades. The crowd oooohed and aaaahhed as the figure showed its duality.

Hades lured the young Persephone with the beautiful side of his mask, keeping the dark side turned away so she didn't see it. The crowd let out a collective gasp as Hades grabbed her and wrenched the basket from her hands. As the flowers spilled over the stage, Hades pulled Persephone into the *skene* and the chorus hummed a low, droning hymn of rape and innocence lost.

Kallistos fanned himself with his hand. The heat bore down on him as the crowd stomped their feet in approval of the abduction scene and awaited Persephone's return. Everyone knew the story—the play was merely another version of it.

Kallistos shifted on his stone seat. Sophocles sat

farther to the left, his head resting on his hand, sleeping. He clearly wasn't worried about Silas's plays.

Suddenly, Persephone appeared on the roof of the *skene*. Kallistos knew it was through a trap door, but the effect was shocking, nonetheless. It was as if the underworld spit her out onto the land. The actor was sideways and pretended to pick flowers on the roof, stumbling as he did so. He made his way to the side of the roof then turned to come back. The crowd gasped.

The mask, so beautiful and feminine, was now split. One side was dark and mangled—like Hades's face. Her transformation was complete and now she was seen for what she'd become. She had failed to hold true and would now suffer in the underworld for part of the year.

The crowd yelled and stomped approval.

Kallistos shuddered. Silas had done a fantastic job with the play and his actors had acted well. The masks' incidents in the first two plays were forgotten. Overall, Persephone was a solid performance with a bonus for the shock the masks had on the audience.

The actors came out for their goodbyes and most everyone in the *theatron* rose to their feet and yelled their appreciation for the entertaining spectacle. Silas had done well, there was no question.

"Yours is still better," Stephanos yelled over the din.

"We have yet to see Sophocles's minotaur."

The circular pool lay in the middle of the gymnasium's open bathhouse, surrounded by oil lamps and flickering torches. Alexios left his tunic in the larger changing area with the attendants, and coolness breezed over his naked body as he walked through the chilly night air. He shivered before sliding into the warm water, eyes closed.

Silas's plays had been good, but not spectacular. Sophocles needn't worry about him. And he wasn't.

Only two of Silas's masks had broken, even though he was sure Mattan had sabotaged them all, as planned. Maybe the crew had discovered the issue and fixed the masks before the performance.

Alexios moved his arms slowly under the water, sending ripples of warmth across his torso. He could do the same damage to Kallistos's masks, but Sophocles wanted a larger sabotage. Something what would assure Sophocles's win.

Kallistos's plays were rumored to be much better than Silas's. He'd had a lot of local success before he was chosen to write plays for Dionysia, and Alexios was sure that Sophocles had reason to worry. Disrupting Kallistos's plays wasn't going to be easy—especially since he didn't even know anything about them yet. Part of him struggled with sabotaging Kallistos. Yet he wanted to make sure the beautiful one wasn't hurt, so he needed to be the one handling Sophocles's dirty work.

Alexios gazed out over the bath area at the dozens of naked men who had come to relax after the day's festivities. A few had likely played sports before heading to the bathhouse, but most probably came directly from the feast. Some were in the water, and some relaxed on long benches around the perimeter of the pool, talking and debating in the cool, night air. Evenings provided a respite from the warm festival days, and the pool added an additional means of relaxation for the exhausted revelers.

Several were getting olive-oil massages on the long, stone tables that lined the side wall. Any other time, Alexios would have savored the bath and watching the naked men too. He didn't come to Athens as often as he would like and there wasn't a fancy bathhouse or gymnasium in his small town—plus Athens was heating the pool water for the festival, which made the baths even more wonderful.

Usually the plunge pool was cold. Invigorating, but cold. A warm bath in such a large pool was a treat, even in Athens. The starry sky domed above him, laying out a sparkling mat that looked almost exactly the same as his view from the hillside while tending sheep. In Athens, the stars seemed to blaze more brightly—lighting the way to his future on the city's stage.

The peace that came with meditation in the countryside couldn't be replaced by the bustle of living in Athens, but if he wanted to be an actor of any note, he'd have to move to the city.

And that took money. Or a wealthy benefactor.

He closed his eyes and slipped his head under the water. The warmth soothed his muscles and he couldn't help but let a sigh bubble out when he resurfaced. The mumbling of ten conversations faded as he leaned against the curved side of the pool and sat on the stone seat that lined the wall around the pool. A musician gently plucked his lyre and the melody floated out over the steamy water, reverberating across the placid surface.

"Sorry."

Alexios opened his eyes as an older man slid next to him on the seat. The man smiled and tilted his head.

"Not interested." Alexios scooted away and turned from the man. The man moved to find another target across the pool.

Young boys dumped heated water into the pool at various places, hoping to maintain the bath at a comfortable temperature. The warmer water swirled around him and steam rose from its surface in places. The large urns of hot water sloshed as they returned from the fires outside and the boys dodged all shapes of men entering and exiting the pool.

Alexios smiled. When he was a wealthy actor, he'd have a warm-water bath in his home, and maybe even a salt water pool too.

A light-haired man caught his attention in the torchlight, and he froze. Kallistos, clad only in a cotton wrap from his waist to his knees, looked out over the pool edge. For a moment, he hesitated, seeming to reconsider the bath, then he pulled the wrap free and handed it to an attendant.

Alexios drew in a breath so strongly that he felt he might faint from lightheadedness. The beautiful one was a well-earned nickname. Kallistos stood tall and lean, his waist narrow and his shoulders wide over trim, muscular hips. His legs were lightly muscled and the light hair that covered them gleamed in the humid air.

Alexios ran his tongue over his lips, making an effort not to stare open-mouthed as he gazed at Kallistos's cock burrowed in a nest of fine, light hair. His own cock responded instantly as he was sure a dozen more responded around him. Kallistos could have modeled for sculpture without a second of hesitation.

Kallistos's eyes locked on Alexios. Alexios blushed and pushed the wet hair from his face. Would he join him, or enter the water elsewhere?

Kallistos smiled, and the warmth spread throughout his face, lighting it up from within. Everyone in the bathhouse watched him as if a god had walked into the mortals' midst. He commanded attention, even just walking. What would it take to break through to him, to gain his trust?

Kallistos entered the water from the far side of the pool, the smile still on his face. The water lapped at his waist and rippled in concentric circles around him as he moved through the pool toward Alexios.

Alexios gulped. How would he hide his condition? He was nude and sure as Hades didn't have anything to cover himself with. He crossed his legs, but the ache Kallistos had set in motion wasn't going away without serious effort. Preferably with Kallistos. His groin surged at the thought.

"Alexios!"

"Kallistos. It's good to see you." Too good. He didn't stand but sank deeper in the water.

"I hoped I would see you today, but you didn't seek me out at the *theatron*. May I sit with you for a while?"

Alexios nodded, hoping the semidarkness would help mask his hard-on. Surely it was an issue men faced at the pools, but he'd never had to deal with it. At least the water was warm.

Kallistos sat beside him, shoulder to shoulder, and his wake of warm water slid over Alexios like a velvet touch. He was pretty sure he moaned, but Kallistos didn't react.

"What did you think of Silas's plays today?" Kallistos ran his wet hand through his hair, darkening the light blond locks and forming them into heavy waves curling at his shoulders.

"I…umm…liked them fine. *Persephone* was the best one but I left as soon as it was over. I wanted to run at the gymnasium to get some exercise after all the wine I've had in the last few days."

Kallistos laughed. "There's been a lot of wine."

"Yes, and I get restless if I don't exercise. I ran, then got dressed. But when I saw that the plunge pool was heated, I decided to relax a while." He pushed at the water and swirled it, hoping the movement would conceal his excitement.

"I wanted to leave right after the play too, but I was obligated to make an appearance and also to congratulate Silas." Kallistos leaned in, his wet shoulder brushing Alexios's. "I'll admit, my mind wasn't on the plays today."

Alexios trembled and heat coursed through him. How had they switched places? Kallistos confident and he acting like a nervous child? "What were you thinking about?"

"My plays. Props, actors, Sophocles."

Alexios froze. Did Kallistos know about Sophocles's trickery? It seemed that every man in the pool stared at them, but on second glance, Alexios realized it was his mind tricking him.

"And I thought about you." Kallistos ducked his head.

"Oh?" Alexios waited for an indication that Kallistos would speak more. If he knew about the plans, he wouldn't be sitting in the pool with him, being friendly. He watched Kallistos's moist mouth form silent words as he stumbled over what to say.

"I couldn't get you out of my mind."

"Me?" Alexios whispered.

"Meeting you. Our time together. Our kisses."

"I'm glad we met."

"So am I. It feels fated, in some odd way. But you don't believe in the Fates."

One of the youths poured in hot water near him, and the heated water spread out over his thighs like a caress. "It's certainly a happy coincidence. If it is the Fates I have to thank, then I do so gladly."

Alexios uncrossed his legs and splashed water over his face to ease the burning there. Kallistos had no idea how much he tormented him, even with merely his eager philosophy. His good looks just completed everything.

"I'm often not comfortable with other people, except on stage. With you, I feel an ease I'm not used to. It is…unusual." Kallistos stared up at the stars. The torchlight lit his face with warmth and softness.

"And I feel as if we are old friends."

"Yes. I thought a lot about our conversation," Kallistos continued. "About what happens after death. About the existence of the gods."

"Oh?"

"Yes. You've given me reason to explore ideas and philosophies that I hadn't taken time to examine before." He put his hand on Alexios's thigh.

"I'm glad," Alexios said. A trail of underwater shivers raced from his thigh to his abdomen.

"And I agree with you. As free-minded men, we have to go after our desires. We shouldn't hold back." He tightened his grip on Alexios's thigh and inched up his leg.

"It is our obligation," Alexios panted.

"We only live one time on this land, as far as we know. And even if I am going to spend eternity in Hades, I want to make the most of my life here. Now."

He gazed into Alexios's eyes, his hand stopping just below the place Alexios most wanted it.

Alexios submitted to the stare, and Kallistos peered into his inner depths, peeling away the layers to the heart of his essence. Passion boiled in his gut, and he knew all it would take was one look in the water for Kallistos to see exactly how he felt. The thought both excited and frightened him. "Men shouldn't be bound by social convention."

"Agreed."

"What is it you want, Kallistos?" The words felt as if they came from his core, and his voice hitched as he spoke them. His whole body tingled—anticipation, desire, and fear of Kallistos finding out his debt to Sophocles, intertwined. A heady experience.

Kallistos's eyes blazed. "I want this." He leaned in and wrapped his arms around Alexios's neck and pulled him into a wet kiss. The warm water sloshed around them and Alexios relaxed in Kallistos's arms.

Damn Sophocles. Damn him for his need to win. Damn him for his old ways and his enslavement of men. Damn him to Hades.

Kallistos's tongue slid into his mouth and he pushed back, ravenous. He fought for control, then settled into sharing the kiss equally. Kallistos nipped at his chin and ran his smooth cheek over the curve of Alexios's jaw. The pool surroundings faded into oblivion and all that existed was the beautiful one's mouth on his chin, his neck, and his own mouth. He was sure that some watched, but he didn't care.

Let them be jealous.

Finally, Kallistos drew back, and Alexios whimpered. Kallistos grinned then slid his hand higher, and firmly grasped Alexios's cock.

KALLISTOS STROKED AND SQUEEZED. His own cock begged to be touched but he ignored the throbbing and worked on Alexios. He'd rather have had him out in the open air, in private, where he could feel each bump and ridge, but for now, this felt right. He needed to possess this man who brought him to his knees with both passion and philosophy.

Though it was common to see people having sex in public, he'd never been one to want an audience. Right now, he didn't care.

Right now, he needed Alexios.

Alexios closed his eyes. His dark, wet lashes splayed against his olive skin and Kallistos leaned forward and kissed each eyelid.

"Do you like it when I stroke you?" he whispered.

Alexios nodded, his mouth half open. "Yes."

Kallistos leaned in and slipped his tongue between Alexios's parted lips. He kissed him and used his tongue to match the rhythm of his hand strokes.

"You tease me with your kisses and the way your mouth responds to mine." Kallistos pulled away from the kiss. "We're like two parts of a shell, fitting together as one."

Alexios thrust his hips forward, grunting as Kallistos stroked him more forcefully. "Don't stop, please."

"I'm not stopping. I want to feel your pleasure in my hand." He moved faster, sliding into a rhythm just beyond Alexios's ability to keep up.

Kallistos studied Alexios's face, watching for signs he neared climax.

Alexios tensed—that sweet pause before release where the world stops for a moment. He stiffened and his face went slack as he came. Kallistos's heart sped with Alexios's. He moaned, wishing he could feel him better, closer, in a place where others wouldn't see. A place where they could be together with no one near. The two of them.

Giving Alexios one last pull and squeeze, he released him.

"Thank you."

Kallistos leaned closer. "Just seizing the time we have."

Alexios laughed and reached for Kallistos, giving him a few strokes. "Let's get out of here. We are providing a spectacle for free."

"Certainly." Kallistos glanced up and men turned away. Yes, some had watched.

Alexios stood, the water dripping down his chest in rivulets that outlined each muscle. His cock had begun to soften, in that semi-state between arousal and relaxation. Kallistos tugged his own hard cock a few times, savoring Alexios's spent body.

"Hurry," Alexios said.

Kallistos stood, aware that his erection would be visible to everyone in the gymnasium pool area. More than a few men gave him a hungry look or an outright gestured offer.

They grabbed cotton wraps to dry with and moved

toward the smaller rooms at the side of the bathhouse. As Kallistos headed down the hall toward the room he had left his clothing in, Alexios tapped him on the shoulder. "In here," he said, pointing to a small, vacant room.

He looked down the empty hall. "But my clothing is down there in the larger changing room."

Alexios's eyes twinkled. "You don't need it yet." He yanked off Kallistos's cloth and pushed him into the dressing room, pulling the curtain closed behind them.

THE BEAUTIFUL ONE chewed his bottom lip, but his erection showed he was more than just nervous. The room was a bit dark, with light coming underneath and at the top of the curtain—just enough to see his face and the outline of his body. Perfect. Alexios dropped his own cloth and shoved Kallistos against the wall, pressing his still-damp muscles against the beautiful one's chest. Kallistos wrapped his arms around Alexios's back and pulled him close.

Alexios rubbed against Kallistos's body, his cock buzzing at the contact with Kallistos's very hard one. It felt so good to feel him, nakedness to nakedness, nothing between them. He pushed his tongue into

Kallistos's mouth, hard. Kallistos tried to keep up, but Alexios led—plundering the man's mouth with his own. He nipped at his chin, then his neck. Kallistos lay his head back against the wall and panted as Alexios tweaked his nipples with his lips.

"I want you in my mouth," Alexios growled. Kallistos nudged his hips forward and it was all the permission Alexios needed. He dropped to his knees. He moved forward, then buried his head in the wet, soft hair between Kallistos's legs.

Kallistos stiffened and his cock bobbed. Alexios wasn't going to make it that easy. He ran his tongue around the man's balls, licking them over and again until Kallistos collapsed against the wall, his breathing ragged and heavy, his hands in Alexios's hair.

When he finally closed his lips over Kallistos's length, they both moaned. Alexios savored the salty taste and the steady pulsing in his mouth, then sucked.

Kallistos barely stood, holding himself up against the wall, thrusting his cock into Alexios's mouth again and again. Alexios took him deep into his throat. He pulled him deeper, trying to get him completely into his mouth. When Kallistos tensed, Alexios stroked him hard as he came, taking everything into his mouth and swallowing. Kallistos sagged and Alexios licked him clean, nuzzling and kissing as he did so.

"What's going on here?" Mattan opened the curtain and peered into the room.

"Mattan!" Alexios pulled back and wiped his mouth as he stood. Mattan could ruin everything. Kallistos tried to hide his groin with his hands, and then stepped behind Alexios, using him as cover.

"Who is he?" Kallistos asked. He put his hands on Alexios's shoulders and leaned against his back.

"How did you find me?" A low burn crept from Alexios's stomach to his mouth.

"Everyone saw you two leave the pool." Mattan looked at Kallistos. "I'm Alexios's friend. He knows me well." He peered around Alexios to get a glimpse of Kallistos. Kallistos cowered. "Not as well as he knows you, though. By the looks of things."

Alexios stifled a growl. "Go away, Mattan. I'm busy."

"Yes. That's obvious. I gave you a bit of time before I followed, but I need to talk to you."

"Later."

"You'll talk to me now. Get dressed and meet me outside the training room."

Alexios shook his head in defeat. If Mattan needed him so urgently, Sophocles must be worried.

He'd better go talk to Mattan, otherwise he might tell Kallistos about Sophocles. "Kallistos, I have to go. It's about employment, and I need the work. Opportunities like this don't wait. I'll see you tomorrow, okay?"

"But…" Kallistos backed away.

"Please, trust me." Alexios pulled him close. "Tomorrow, my love." He pressed his lips to Kallistos's and felt the freefall that accompanied their kisses. "Right now, I have to go. I promise, we'll be together soon."

SIX

*R*uddy mid-afternoon sunlight streamed across the stage and lit the amphitheater seats, casting shadows of the roaring crowd across the hillside like rows of waving grain. Kallistos gazed over the cheering throng. Thus far, Sophocles's plays had been brilliant, as expected.

Kallistos stretched his legs out then adjusted the pillow under him on the stone seat. The best was yet to come—Sophocles's golden minotaur would make its appearance in the final play. Sophocles had made sure to spread the word so that everyone knew to expect something phenomenal.

It had worked.

The excitement from the crowd rolled down the hill and over Kallistos like a heavy blanket. Tension knotted his shoulders and he fidgeted with the edge of his tunic, picking at the loose threads.

Bion and Diokles sat to his left and Stephanos to his right, surely as nervous as Kallistos was, but none of them showed it at all. Kallistos slumped in his seat, his stomach roiling. The waiting was slowly killing him.

His thoughts drifted to Alexios and the evening in the pool. Would he and Alexios continue what they had begun after the festival, or would their connection be lost on the wind? He didn't know. If he had his way, he'd choose to be with the shepherd. But Alexios hadn't spoken of a lasting relationship.

"The crowd loves him," Bion said. He ran his hand through his short, dark hair.

"Yes," Diokles said. "My acting won't rival his skilled players."

"We have passion." Kallistos straightened in his seat. "We have a chance." He rubbed his stomach to soothe away the uneasiness. The past few days had been both challenging and exhilarating, and meeting Alexios had flipped his life—and his plans—upside down. He should have been spending the time preparing for his plays instead of philosophizing in the gymnasium. And kissing.

And…. His face warmed.

"Here he comes," Stephanos said. He leaned forward in his seat and Kallistos followed his gaze. The actors and sponsors sat close to the stage, but the crowd roared so loudly when Sophocles appeared that there was no chance of hearing him, even from the short distance away. Dust rose in the air as wind brushed over the stage, and the particles glinted and sparkled as the sun touched them.

Sophocles, his longer actor's robes fluttering, tipped his head at the crowd, acknowledging the cheers and adulation without addressing them directly. The crowd shouted his name and stomped the ground.

The City Dionysia wouldn't be the same without Sophocles.

Kallistos scanned the faces in the crowd in an attempt to locate Alexios among the thousands. He was out there somewhere, but lost in the sea of faces. Kallistos know he was in attendance, because he'd wanted to see Sophocles in action as much as the rest of Athens. After the rumors circulated about the minotaur, no one would miss the play unless they had a dire reason. In fact, most of the people who traveled to Athens from afar for the Great Dionysia came to see the playwright's skill.

And imbibe the free wine.

Sophocles held his hands into the air and the crowd stilled. He paused a moment then said, in a deep voice meant to carry the breadth of the theater, "For your pleasure and terror—Minos and the golden minotaur." Before the crowd could erupt in cheers, the small chorus began chanting and Sophocles slipped into the *skene*. The air almost crackled with anticipation.

Kallistos took a deep breath and leaned forward on his seat, the hairs on his forearms standing alert. Would this one play eclipse everything he'd prepared so many months for? Had his work been for naught?

A lone actor entered the stage and walked across the expansive dirt floor, his royal robes trailing behind him. He didn't speak.

King Minos.

The chorus sang of his wife Pasiphae's lust for one of Poseidon's great bulls—a white specimen larger than all others. As they told the story, verse by verse, Minos clasped his hands behind his back and paced, head down as if in deep thought. His mask glowed stark white with black paint around the eyes and exaggerated eyebrows that dipped in an angry curve.

Kallistos crossed his arms to keep them from shaking. His lunch threatened to spill, and he fought the nausea, trying to relax. He was used to being nervous around people, but not because of a play.

The chorus continued, singing of the replica cow that Pasiphae used to copulate with the white bull. When they sang of the minotaur's conception, their voices trebled high and loud over the crowd. King Minos, who, judging by his height and build, was played by Sophocles himself, paced the stage, growing more and more agitated as the story went on—wringing his hands and shaking his head.

When the chorus sang of the minotaur's birth, King Minos dropped to the ground, holding his heart and groaning, as if he'd been struck by a spear. The crowd stomped their approval at the dramatic representation of betrayal.

King Minos disappeared into the *skene*. As the chants grew louder and more forceful, the *skene* door burst open and the minotaur thundered onto the stage.

The crowd gasped, then screamed and stomped as the minotaur rushed the altar and jumped on it. His golden mask gleamed in the sunlight. It was likely visible from the Acropolis.

Kallistos realized his mouth hung open. He snapped it shut then glanced at Bion and Diokles. Both sat immobile, stunned. He turned to Stephanos, who was shaking his head slowly, his mouth drawn in a firm line and his eyes wide.

The minotaur posed on the altar. The mask must have weighed a lot because it rested on the actor's shoulders and he slumped, even though he appeared to be a large, muscular man. Gemstones gleamed from their settings —red stones around the mouth and blues and greens around the eyeholes. The two spiral horns were each topped by a large pearl set directly into the gold. The minotaur turned and his purple silk robes shimmered as the diaphanous material fluttered in the slight breeze.

What must it have cost to craft something so fine? Kallistos's benefactor was wealthy, but he certainly didn't have that amount of money to spare. Everyone in the *theatron* gaped at the magnificent sight. Most would have never seen such a display of wealth, other than at the temples. For a mere mortal to showcase so much gold was unheard of.

Sophocles knew that well.

The minotaur tipped its head back and roared. The actor playing the part was huge and his lungs strong —his roars broke the stunned silence and echoed over the hillside in waves. For a moment, all was silent. Then, some in the crowd snarled back and soon the whole crowd roared and spit, mimicking the beast on stage. The minotaur pawed the air with his large hands and jumped off the altar and ran along the stage, continuing to roar and threaten.

The crowd loved it.

The play continued, portraying King Minos's banishment of the minotaur to the dark and puzzling labyrinth. The sacrifices of seven Athenian girls and seven Athenian boys played out in great detail. Some in the crowd shielded their eyes as the golden minotaur hunted and devoured his prey but others watched the blood sport before their eyes.

Theseus appeared on top of the *skene* through some trapdoor that Silas had made use of for Persephone and peered down onto the stage where the minotaur lumbered through his labyrinth, golden mask shining. Theseus spoke of killing the beast and freeing Athens from the Minoan pact—no more Athenian youths would be sent to their deaths in the minotaur's maze. He shouted and the crowd responded with chants of, "Athens! Athens!"

A stagehand tossed a ball of twine from the trapdoor to Theseus. Although he only glimpsed him briefly, he looked like the man who had pulled Alexios away from him at the gymnasium the night before. Mattan? Did he work for Sophocles? If so, what was Alexios doing talking to him about employment?

Theseus tied the twine to a post on the *skene* roof and climbed down a ladder onto the stage, trailing the twine behind him. He tied the twine from post to post, tracing his steps as he hunted the minotaur. The crowd hung on the edges of their seats, waiting for the final confrontation. Kallistos watched, completely absorbed in the play.

Theseus found the minotaur sleeping in front of the altar and he dropped the twine and crouched beside the beast. The minotaur lay still, his golden mask unmoving.

Theseus called out to the minotaur, challenging him to fight, but there was no response. The chorus chanted louder as Theseus approached the sleeping minotaur. As soon as Theseus raised a rock, the beast roared awake and jumped to his feet. The crowd cheered for Theseus—chanting his name.

The minotaur attacked Theseus and they fought, hand-to-hand, around the stage, taking care to stay within the twined sections. The crowd gasped as the minotaur struck Theseus down, then shouted as Theseus rose to fight again. Again and again, Theseus went down and again and again, he got back up.

Kallistos's heart thumped. How would he compete with this show of brilliance?

Finally, with a savage blow to the head, the minotaur lay dead. Theseus straddled him, arms in the air, victorious. He raised the golden mask into the air like a trophy.

Athens was safe.

The applause and stomping went on for what seemed like forever, and Kallistos rose and stared out to the mountains in the distance. Sophocles had shown the greatest city in the world the greatest spectacle they had ever seen. And he had to follow the next day with his own plays.

ALEXIOS WAITED IN THE *AGORA*. He'd rushed out of the *theatron* as soon as Sophocles's plays ended, in hopes of catching Kallistos on his way home. He had the food basket packed. Kallistos had to say yes—he had to talk to him. After the evening in the gymnasium, there were things left to finish.

The crowd swarmed from the stands, laughing and chattering about the success of Sophocles's plays. The minotaur had been unbelievable, amazing, incredible—the crowd spoke of it all.

Sophocles had the valuable mask guarded by two men at all times. They'd stayed backstage in the *skene* while the actor performed, but at all other times they were with the mask. Alexios had stayed backstage and helped with costume changes, where Kallistos wouldn't see him.

While the crowd had roared its approval of Sophocles, Alexios had time to think. His time helping Sophocles was nearly over, and he was finished doing the old man's bidding.

Kallistos deserved to have a fair chance at winning. No matter the consequences, tonight he would tell Kallistos everything. Alexios couldn't live with himself knowing he was only acting on stage because he'd ruined someone else's dreams. As much as he wanted to be a famous actor, he wasn't going to sacrifice his integrity. He'd been blinded by the temptation, but Kallistos shown him the truth.

Where was Kallistos?

He should have come out of the *theatron* by this point. The crowd had thinned some as many had made their way toward the *agora*. How would Kallistos take the news? Alexios could only hope that he would forgive him. He hadn't actually done anything to hurt him yet—other than lie about everything.

Ugh. Alexios shook his head. If Kallistos forgave him, it would be a miracle. They had bonded so deeply in just a few days—maybe he would understand that Alexios had a moment of weakness where selfishness ruled his actions. Regardless, Alexios couldn't hurt Kallistos. He cared about him deeply, and no matter what the reward from Sophocles would be, it wouldn't be enough.

It could never be enough.

As the rest of the babbling crowd pushed by, Alexios saw a blond head in the distance. Kallistos, with his actors and benefactor, headed toward the wine stands. Alexios swallowed. Hopefully things would go well, and he would have Kallistos in his life forever. He grabbed his basket and headed to catch him before he reached the lines for wine.

"Kallistos," he called. The basket scraped against his leg and he hefted it to the other hand. A man shoved by him, knocking him off-balance.

Kallistos turned and smiled, his whole face lighting up. "Alexios. It's good to see you."

"And you, my love."

Kallistos blushed and he looked to see if his actors heard the remark, but they were caught up in their own conversation with Stephanos.

"We need to talk. Away from here." Alexios

shifted the basket in his hands. "Will you join me for dinner?"

"I'd be happy to. You're spoiling me with your kindness in bringing meals to me."

"I love dining outside," Alexios said. "It is made even better when you join me. And we both have to eat." He thought about all the lonely days he spent eating meals out in the pastures. Hopefully, those days were behind him now.

"Bion, Diokles, don't forget that we need to move our props tonight." Kallistos nudged one of the men.

The actors turned. "Meet you at Stephanos's house this evening."

"I'll see you there, Bion," Kallistos said. He brushed off the front of his tunic and Alexios watched the way his hand moved over the fabric, sweeping just the top. How he wanted to run his own hands over that chest and feel the sold muscle the fabric enclosed.

The actors walked off into the crowd with Stephanos, already reengaged in their interrupted conversation. Kallistos turned to Alexios and put his hand on his shoulder, giving it a rub and squeeze, sending a wave of shivers down Alexios's arm. "I've missed you, even though it hasn't even been a day."

"I've longed for you too."

"You left so quickly with that man, Mattan, last night. I would've liked to spend more time together."

"As would I. I had to talk to him, though." Alexios shifted the basket to the other hand. "We had business to discuss."

"I saw him working props during Sophocles's minotaur play."

"Maybe. Sophocles no doubt hires many helpers." Alexios' stomach clenched. He couldn't tell Kallistos yet. They needed to be alone, where he could explain everything. Nonetheless, he hated lying for one moment longer.

Kallistos nodded. The volume near the *agora* had grown to a near ear-shattering level as everyone convened in the square. Dancing had already started, and the acrobats were out on the street again, entertaining and bringing laughs.

"Let's go somewhere quiet," Alexios said, nearly shouting. "I know a place just outside the city."

Kallistos nodded, his golden hair falling forward over his face. He brushed it back with his hand and smiled. Alexios's groin warmed.

He took Kallistos's hand and led him out of the crowded *agora* and through the streets of Athens. They walked without speaking, holding hands and taking in the sights and smells of festival. Floral garlands draped over doorways and brightly colored fabrics hung on the homes of the wealthy. For a city so often at war, Greater Dionysia always provided Athens a break from strife.

Alexios led Kallistos through the city gates and onto the grassy plain beside the rushing Illisos River. Plane trees towered overhead, bursting with frothy leaves, and grasses waved in the wind. Wildflowers dotted the tops of spindly stems and their fragrant bouquet spread over the meadow.

"I love coming here," Kallistos said, squeezing Alexios's hand. "It is a good place to think."

"I've only been a few times, but the beauty of this place stuck in my memory. I try to come here every time I visit Athens." Indeed, the rushing water soothed his mind when it neared bursting with thought. A perfect place to relax and recoup from the hectic pace of the city. A place to dream and ponder. No wonder Socrates roamed the area with his students —lecturing, philosophizing, and communing.

Kallistos pulled away and made his way nearer to the riverbank where large stones scattered beside the roiling water. "Let's eat over here," he said. "Where we can hear the water splash by."

Alexios joined him, setting the basket on a large, smooth rock that sat close, but not in the river. Two larger boulders shielded the rock and provided privacy from anyone walking by. They stood and tossed pebbles into the water; watching them hit the water and bounce, then disappear into the churning depths. The riverside provided respite to many and solace to almost all—and Alexios hoped it would soothe Kallistos's wounded spirit once he told him of Sophocles's plan.

The high walls that surrounded Athens shielded most of the wind off the meadow, creating a warm, blissful spot to eat. The sunbaked rocks warmed Alexios's hands as he spread the small blanket over the stone. If a better place existed to profess his love for Kallistos, he didn't know where it could be. He smiled at the beautiful one and the dazzling smile he got in return warmed him further.

"The sun will be gone soon," Kallistos said. "And we have no torches."

"We've got a while. Then, we'll share the moonlight."

They sat down, Kallistos hanging his legs over the side of the stone and looking out over the river. Alexios sat behind him, waiting. The evening would be perfect if only he didn't have to reveal his deceit. The revelation of lies would cast a pall over the meadow.

"What are you thinking about?" Alexios asked. He watched Kallistos' shoulders rise and fall and wondered about the tension he must feel—knowing his plays would be onstage the next day. Maybe tonight wasn't the best time to tell him about Sophocles. Maybe he could delay breaking his heart.

"Life, my plays, my desires."

"Heavy topics for dinner."

"You've made me realize that I am a deeper thinker. Not just in my art, but in the life I'm living." Kallistos turned and then moved to face Alexios. "I am so happy when I am around you. I feel alive."

"I am happy too. But aren't you worried about your plays tomorrow?"

Kallistos unpacked the basket. Tonight they would have bread and apples. He set the apples out between them and pulled out a fresh, round loaf of bread.

"I'm not too worried about my plays. We've practiced, and everyone knows their lines. What could go wrong?"

Ice crept through Alexios's veins. What indeed? Though he hadn't planned anything yet, Alexios didn't trust that Sophocles hadn't. Add that to the normal things that could go wrong, like illness or accident, and he realized there were no givens. Even Sophocles could have an accident.

Kallistos picked up an apple and took a bite. "Sophocles's plays were brilliant—I'm not sure I have a chance at winning anyway."

"Of course you do. He was good, I'll agree, but you get to go last, and that makes an impression in itself." Telling Kallistos that Sophocles sent him to sabotage his plays wasn't going to be a simple matter Would he ever forgive him? He sighed and rubbed his face with his hands.

"What's wrong?" Kallistos asked. He reached and touched Alexios on the cheek. "I'm the one that should be worrying, not you."

"I'm just thinking about your plays tomorrow. You mentioned moving your props tonight—is that the final thing?"

"Yes, we plan to roll the horse to the theater late tonight." He took another bite of apple.

"Horse? You are using a live horse?" Alexios leaned in close.

Kallistos froze for a moment. "It's a secret. We're reenacting the Trojan War—the battle between Achilles and Hector."

Alexios picked at the loaf of bread. Kallistos finally trusted him enough to tell him about his plays—right before he would learn of the deception. The Trojan War! What a massive story to tell within one play. How had Kallistos written it?

"Don't you think the war is a good theme for my plays?"

"Yes, everyone loves Achilles." Alexios pulled a chunk of bread from the loaf and popped it into his mouth.

"Except Hector." Kallistos laughed. He tossed the apple core into the river.

"Yes." Alexios returned the laugh. "Except Hector. But where do you think Hector went after his death?"

"I'd think he'd have gone straight to the fields. If they exist. He's a hero too."

"Yes. His death was tragic. But so was Achilles's. Some days I wish the Elysian Fields were a reality." He offered Kallistos the bread, but he shook his head.

"Maybe they are."

"Perhaps. I suppose one day we will know." Alexios stuffed the bread back into the basket. "Will Paris kill Achilles in your play?"

"No. But I do have a secret." Kallistos leaned close. "I built a huge Trojan horse."

"Oh!" Alexios's mind spun. Maybe the old man had been right to worry about Kallistos. He was a threat beyond his writing. "The horse! You actually built the Trojan horse! I thought you meant you had a soldier's mount as a prop."

Kallistos laughed, his voice booming over the river rocks. The late-day sun trumpeted a swath of orange across the river, lighting the air with sparkles.

"How big is it? And where have you hidden it?"

Kallistos smiled. "It is at Stephanos's house, in the back garden. And it is big. Bigger than Athens has seen. We'll roll it to the theater late tonight."

"But how did you build it without anyone seeing it?"

"I'm sure some have seen it, but as far as I know, it is still a secret. We built the entire thing in Stephanos's garden. It took months."

Alexios finally had the information he'd been trying to get for days. Kallistos's third play was about the Trojan War—and he had a prop that truly would rival the golden minotaur mask. He clenched and unclenched his hand. He could ruin Kallistos's plays—it would be easy to have the horse destroyed. He wouldn't even have to do it himself—just let Sophocles know, and it would be taken care of.

He might be the next great actor. But then, he'd be hurting a fellow mortal, and that wasn't acceptable. And the person he would hurt was a man he had grown to care about very deeply in the few days he'd known him. Kallistos was the light to his own dark, the shy to his own outrageousness, the innocence to his trickery.

"What are you thinking about so intently?" Kallistos asked, placing his hand over Alexios's clenched fist. "Why are you upset? You are so tense."

Alexios wavered under the caring touch of his lover. Once Kallistos found out the truth, he wouldn't want to be near him, much less give him a caring caress. Alexios felt like a fraud, someone who deserved to spend eternity in a very dark place. If that was possible. Hot tears trickled down his face. "I'm overwhelmed," he sputtered.

Kallistos pushed the rest of the food and basket out of the way and gripped Alexios in a soft hug. Alexios lay his head on Kallistos' shoulder and wept as the beautiful one stroked his hair. The sun had disappeared, leaving only traces of orange light in the darkening sky. The river coursed beside them in a lullaby of splashes.

"Do you regret your time with me?" Kallistos whispered. "Do you not wish to be with me anymore?"

Alexios pulled out of the hug and wiped the tears from his face. "I want to be with you. The last few days have been the best days I've ever had." It was true. The time he'd spent with Kallistos was not only fun and thoughtful, but had opened up emotions he had rarely felt, and certainly not with another man—contentment, peace, happiness. He could spend the rest of his days with Kallistos and not ever regret the choice.

Stars peeped overhead as night closed over Athens. The Parthenon lit the top of the Acropolis and smoke rose from cooking fires and lamps in the city proper. Alexios felt small, like a lone shepherd with a large flock to defend against the wolves. Only he wasn't alone. Across from him sat the rest of his soul. His heart. Everything that held importance in this cold, harsh world.

"These days have also been special for me."

Alexios sighed. "Forgive my tears. I'm tired from the many days of wine and little sleep."

"A man who shows emotion is to be commended, not condemned."

"Sayeth the wise playwright."

Kallistos scooted to sit at Alexios's side. "An actor must project emotion onstage. The greatest actors pull from their own lives, their own emotions. Even with a mask, he must make the audience feel. Weep. Never be ashamed of feeling. I hid my feelings for so long. You have shown me that it is wrong. To reach the heights of my art, I must live. I must feel. The stage is not where life is lived."

"I hope one day I can be that actor onstage."

"I would be honored if you were in my plays—perhaps next year?"

Perhaps. "I'd like that."

Alexios pushed Kallistos back onto the blanket and lay atop him, his hard body pressing all the right spots. He couldn't tell Kallistos about the deception. Not right now. The props and Trojan horse were safe, and the plays would go on without interruption.

He'd see to it.

This moment here by the river, held magic. He couldn't ruin it. No, he'd wait until after the festival to tell Kallistos.

Kallistos pulled Alexios down into a kiss. Sweet, soft, and with the passion of an actor. Alexios closed his eyes to the moonlight and lost himself in Kallistos's embrace. When their bodies combined, he knew there was nothing more important in this world than the love he felt for the beautiful one.

SEVEN

The horse, covered in drapings, stood tall in Stephanos's back-garden courtyard. Kallistos admired the shape—so solid in the spring moonlight. It had taken many months for the workmen to build the wooden horse, and it had cost Stephanos a lot of money. Now the horse, with its wooden wheels and rope tail, would hide for one more night before being revealed to all of Athens. He patted its leg as if it were a real horse seeking attention.

Kallistos wouldn't be secreting men inside the horse during the play—that would be too complicated. Instead, the horse would roll out into the center of the stage beside the altar. Its grand presence alone should create a stir. Surely everyone would clamor to see it up close after the plays—maybe he'd even wheel it into the *agora* for the day. Even the carpenter, Daedalus, would have been impressed with the creation. From conception, to execution, the horse would stand as one of the greatest props of all time. He hoped.

"Where's Bion?" Kallistos asked. Several servants had been called to move the rolling horse down the streets, and his actors were supposed to be around to help too. He hadn't seen Bion all night.

"I haven't seen him," Diokles said. "He knew to be here."

The servants secured the last drapings around the legs of the horse with thin ropes. Spring florals floated through the night air in the garden. Kallistos sighed, thinking back to lying with Alexios on the warm river stone. The soft touches and easy kisses.

"Want me to go in search of him?"

"No, he knows the plan. He'll find us. Right now, we need to get the horse behind the *skene*."

Diokles grunted in agreement.

Kallistos pulled the heavy garden gate open and the servants huffed as they strained to push the horse. It shuddered as it crept forward. Hopefully, it would withstand its own weight and stay together on the trip to the *theatron*.

"It'll be easier on the flat roads," Kallistos assured. He walked behind, watching the men shove the horse through the gate opening.

Once they made it to the street, the horse moved quietly for such a large contraption, and they pushed it quickly down the road to the theater. The large wheels behind the legs rolled smoothly over the bumps on the dirt road, with only an occasional crackle of rock underneath. Kallistos had chosen the darkest route to the *theatron*—the fewer people who saw the giant prop, the better. Still, they would beg more than a few questions from those who did see them pass by with the rolling behemoth. He'd debated asking Alexios to come help move the horse, but he wanted the prop to be a surprise for him. He wanted him to see it in the daylight, in its place onstage.

"Do you really think we can beat the old man?" Diokles asked. He matched steps with Kallistos and walked beside him as the servants pushed. "His minotaur…"

"I do," Kallistos said. "But it isn't going to be easy." Now that he had met Alexios, he wasn't as consumed to beat the old man, anyway. Sure, he would like to win, for posterity's sake—and he needed to for Stephanos—but his world wasn't going to end if he lost the competition. In fact, a whole new vista was opening up that didn't hinge on how he did in the festival. One he hadn't written a part for. One that included another person—something he never thought would be part of the script of his life.

The sounds of dancing and drinking filled the alleys—echoing from the *agora* and throughout the town as people celebrated another successful day of festival. The town would be oddly quiet in a few days—when the wine and visitors were gone. They passed a few people on the way, most of whom were drunk or otherwise engaged. No one stopped to ask what the giant form was, but he was sure he heard whispers in the semidarkness.

After securing the horse behind the *skene* where it would be hidden from the audience until it rolled out, Kallistos sent all the servants but two back to Stephanos's house. The remaining ones would watch over the horse until daybreak. "You need to find Bion," he told Diokles. "Get Stephanos to help. I'm going to check on our masks and other props then I'll meet you at the house."

"I'll bet he is in the *agora* with a lovely woman," Diokles said, leaning against the *skene* wall. "And a lovely cup of wine." He snickered.

"He can do that business tomorrow night—after our plays. Make sure you don't get distracted either.

You both need to be fresh when the sun joins us in the *theatron* tomorrow." He gazed up at the clad horse, its coverings flapping gently in the wind. Would it be enough to best the famous playwright?

"I'll be ready."

Kallistos nodded and Diokles headed for the gate. Hopefully, Bion would be easy to find in the partying crowd. He might have already gone home while they were moving the horse. Then again, that wasn't too likely, given his affection for women and drink.

He walked around the horse, checking the ties on the coverings and imagining what the crowd's reaction would be when the massive horse rolled out onto the stage. He envisioned thousands of people stomping and chanting his name. He shook his head. Was fame the reason he wrote? Did he just seek confirmation that he was creative? Days ago, it would have been a large part of the reason. Somehow, a man's worth was often measured by his fame and riches rather than his happiness.

The bright moonlight silhouetted the horse against the sky—making it look even taller than it was. Kallistos smiled. Since meeting Alexios, his mind had opened to the possibilities of happiness with another person on a close and intimate level. Not just physical, but emotional and philosophical as well.

He no longer felt the need to hide away completely from human interaction—and he no longer had to interact only on stage. Life could be far more real—and far more emotional. He would never have believed it.

The stars sparkled overhead, and the cool evening breeze swept across his shoulders. He could write plays to showcase his love's talent, and together, they could become a pair that everyone respected. They would share their combined vision with the world, and at the same time, with each other. The world was aligned, and he and Alexios stood in the center. He could finally say that he was truly happy and unafraid of what the future would bring.

He pulled the backdoor to the *skene* open and stepped inside. The oily smoke from lamps hung heavily in the air, and the corridor looked much narrower in the dim light. Who would be here tonight? Maybe Sophocles had people removing his lesser props.

Certainly, the golden mask was safe at his home and ready to display as a winning trophy. He'd probably have a parade for the mask when festival was over.

Pushing aside the fabric curtain, he slipped into his props' room, not wanting to have to talk to anyone. He'd check to see that all the masks and other props were in order, then go back to Stephanos's house to try to sleep.

The only light in his room came from the moonlight through the high windows. Still, he could make out the masks, just as he'd left them. One, two, three, four…yes, they were all here and ready. Wooden swords leaned against the wall and miscellaneous other props were displayed and ready for use. *Amphoras* of wine sat on the table and plates sat ready for fruit and bread. There wasn't anything left to do.

Everything was in place, including the horse. Now he had to wait for morning. And find Bion.

He heard a mumbling in the hallway, and then a gruff voice.

"Unacceptable," the man said.

The voice sounded familiar and he strained to hear more, leaning against the wall.

"He isn't going to be happy," the voice continued. "You've failed."

Mattan! Had he come to retrieve Sophocles's props?

"But I tried," came another voice.

Alexios! Why was Alexios with Mattan? Kallistos eased over to stand beside his curtained doorway, careful not to disturb the fabric and give away his position. Mattan wasn't someone who he wanted to be around. Why was Alexios with him yet again? What business could they possibly have at this hour? And what had Alexios failed at?

"Sophocles doesn't accept tried," Mattan growled. "Kallistos's plays must fail. Your job—and you agreed. No excuses."

Kallistos's heart went cold, as if an icy dagger had slit his chest from neck to groin—and Alexios had plunged the blade. He couldn't move, couldn't breathe, and he gripped the wall to steady himself. Plays must fail...

"Sophocles did well enough with his own plays. Why must he cheat?" He could hear the pleading in Alexios's voice. No matter. He hadn't been forced. Must fail...

"Don't try to be ethical now. You agreed to the terms," Mattan said.

"But—"

"Too late. Forget being an actor, shepherd boy. Your fate is sealed. Pack your stuff and go back to your sheep."

Someone stomped off and Kallistos heard the *skene* door slam closed. Tears rushed his eyes. Alexios had feigned love just to get close enough to sabotage the plays? Everything they shared had been a ruse? To get an acting part? He choked on his tears and coughed. How had he misread Alexios so much? He bumped against one of the prop swords and it clattered to the ground.

"Who's in here?" Alexios asked, poking his head into the room, carrying one of Sophocle's masks and a handful of actors' robes.

"Get out," Kallistos bit out, tears flowing freely now. His heart squeezed out painful beats.

Alexios's eyes grew wide as he must have realized that Kallistos had overheard the conversation with Mattan. "I must explain—"

"I heard everything. There's nothing to say," Kallistos said, barely above a whisper. His stomach quivered with rage. "I should never have opened my heart to you."

He stormed to the doorway, and Alexios stepped in front of him as he tried to pass. He dropped the mask and robes and reached for Kallistos, tears falling from his eyes.

"I love you," Alexios said. "I would never hurt you." His face showed horror and pleading, but to Kallistos, he was pure treachery.

"You love yourself," Kallistos said. "And money.

Let me go now and at least have the dignity of walking away from you and your deceit."

Alexios bowed his head, weeping, and stepped aside. Kallistos slipped by and headed into the night.

ALEXIOS PACED in his room at Sophocles's house. His straw mattress lay in the corner of the room giving him plenty of space to move about and he used it all as he walked to and fro. He had lit a small lamp, and he watched it shake as he strode by.

The look on Kallistos's face was one he would have wished to never see. Ever. Complete sadness—all the way to his heart. He was a broken man, and it was Alexios's fault. He sighed and smacked his palms against his forehead repeatedly. Why had he agreed to help Sophocles? What manner of selfishness had taken him so completely? Now everything was ruined.

Kallistos would never speak to him again, never kiss him, never touch him. He'd never get the chance to discuss philosophy with him again, or relax in the gymnasium pool after a round of exercise. No, Alexios would go back to tending sheep and spend the rest of his life dreaming about the beautiful one and the missed opportunity for love.

"Alexios!" Mattan shouted from outside the doorway. He came around the corner and stood, arms crossed. "Out. He wants you out of his house. You are no longer welcome."

"What?"

"Out. You didn't think he'd allow a traitor to stay, did you? You're lucky all he is doing is making you leave."

"I'm no traitor."

"You're a traitor of the worst sort. You support the enemy."

Alexios sighed. He was a traitor. To himself, and to Kallistos. He grabbed his sack and stuffed the few things he'd brought inside, then tied it up. He could be out of Sophocles's house in a few minutes, and he'd be sure never to enter it again.

Mattan watched silently, leaning against the wall, his raspy breath growing stronger with each moment that passed. "Hurry up," he said. "I have things to do besides watch over a traitor."

Alexios grabbed his money pouch, with the few coins he had left. Not enough to stay at an inn—he'd sleep on the streets tonight, and tomorrow he'd head home to the sheep, the stars, and the silent, open sky.

He'd continue to philosophize with the night, alone—knowing he had totally ruined his chances at love, or an acting job in any reputable play. Maybe he'd attend Kallistos's performance, maybe not. Sophocles would still try to ruin the plays. He wasn't sure he could bear the disappointment Kallistos would suffer.

Mattan followed him outside into the chilly night air. "I told you you'd never be an actor, sheep boy. Go back to your herd. Let them keep you company in the night."

Alexios ground his teeth together and walked away. The last thing he needed to do was end up in a fight with Mattan. Thankfully, Sophocles always had someone else do his dirty work—it was easier to hear the truth from Mattan. It seemed fitting, somehow. He was no better than Mattan—he'd sold his heart for the promise of fame.

He headed toward the *agora* to grab some free wine and find a place to sleep. Fortunately, many slept in the streets during festival, and no one would give him a second look. Sheep boy, he had always been, and sheep boy, he would remain.

EIGHT

I'm ruined.

Kallistos paced the props' room. The first play had gone relatively well—Helen had been whisked away by Paris in a dramatic scene with the chorus chanting and singing verses of betrayal. The crowd had stomped their approval, and no one had thrown things at the stage. Diokles had acted well—his Helen svelte—and he might even have convinced a drunken Athenian that he was female, he moved so well in the costume.

The crowd outside chattered and the sound vibrated through the *skene* walls, mirroring the chattering of his teeth. There wasn't a lot of time to relax—he was expected onstage for the last play at any moment, depending on the length of the crowd's acclamation. He moved the props needed for the last play to the front of the room. Diokles and the servants were taking the bindings off the horse and getting it into position to roll out.

The second play had been more difficult than the abduction of Helen. Bion had not shown up at the *theatron*. He'd not even slept at the house. Stephanos had men out looking for him all night, but Kallistos and Diokles ended up doubling up and switching out roles to perform the second play—the siege of Troy and Patroclus's valiant death while wearing Achilles's armor. The *theatron* was the setup for the third and final play—the finale—and the timing had been off with all the mask changes because of Bion's absence.

Where is he?

Kallistos lay his head against the wall and nearly wept. What else could go badly? Not only had he been betrayed by Alexios, but now he couldn't perform the third play. His version of the story had Achilles, Hector, and Odysseus onstage all at once— and that would be impossible with only two actors.

Maybe he shouldn't have changed the historical timeline—and not had Odysseus show up with Hector and Achilles at all.

He could've ended with the fight between Achilles and Hector and then Bion's absence wouldn't pose a problem. It was too late now—he needed the horse if he had any chance of winning, and Odysseus was the one who would wrap up the play. He'd have to fight a ghost Hector, unless Bion got to the *theatron*.

If only he'd had an extra day—he could have trained someone to step into the role. As it was, the play was ruined.

He pulled his Achilles mask on, buckled his prop armor, and picked up his wooden sword. He'd have to improvise; though fighting an imaginary Hector was likely to look comedic rather than tragic. At the *skene* doors, he took a deep breath then nodded to the servants.

They pushed the doors open, and sunlight streamed into his eyes, momentarily blinding him to the whole of Athens, awaiting his play. He stepped out onto the dirt stage. The crowd stomped and the echo thundered around him—ricocheting off the sides of the *skene*.

Up to this point, he hadn't really taken in how many people were in attendance. The theater held over sixteen thousand, and the seating area was filled.

How many people would he disappoint with his imaginary Hector? How many would jeer at his failed performance? One of the many was Alexios—he would be somewhere in the crowd. Whether he jeered or cried was no matter. It was time to perform.

He gazed to where Sophocles sat, smiling. It was as if he knew Kallistos was on the verge of disaster. The old man would win again and wear the laurel leaves of victory in his gray hair.

Too bad the winner's crown didn't have goat horns like the priests' headdresses did. To top it off, he'd have to sit and watch Sophocles' satyr play and pretend he was happy for the man—all the while knowing he was a cheat and a fraud. If he went to the *archon*, he'd be labeled petty.

No one would ever believe that the great Sophocles was a cheat.

With a quavering voice, he announced his play and the crowd responded with stomps and cheers. He savored the moment—knowing the fickle people would soon turn on him and he would be ridiculed and laughed at. How quickly things could change.

He stepped toward the altar and raised his wooden sword—the cue for the chorus to begin singing the song of Achilles' sadness over the death of his lover, Patroclus. The irony overcame him, and tears streamed down his face under the mask. Achilles had lost Patroclus, and he had lost Alexios. Tragedy was real life.

A cooing white dove landed on the altar, its head bobbing as it took in the scene. He waved it away with his sword. Aphrodite's bird had brought only trouble and heartache.

Love's promise was fleeting.

He walked his cues and performed his sadness for the crowd as the chorus ramped up their song in preparation for Hector to come through the Gates of Troy to battle Achilles.

He knew his sorrow reached the people and wrapped around their hearts—he heard many sobs and shouts of condolence for Achilles. Never once had his acting been so parallel to reality. If only he had a Hector to battle, then the play might succeed.

With a deep sigh, he raised his sword in both hands and turned to face the *skene* doors and the phantom Hector. Would the crowd laugh at his pantomime? Would they know what was happening? He hadn't had time to change the chorus' lines—but hopefully they would tell the story clearly enough.

The doors parted and Hector stood tall in the doorway. The crowd stomped and Kallistos's heart leapt.

Bion!

Hector approached, his sword drawn. His mask, painted in stark colors, gave him an almost evil appearance. To Athens, he was the villain—dark and foreboding and not of the city. Troy was the enemy and always portrayed in darkness. Achilles was light and heroic—white and golden.

"You killed Patroclus, my friend and lover!" Achilles yelled, waving his sword in the air. "You will suffer!"

The men circled, swords waving.

"Bion, where were you?" Kallistos whispered as he leaned in for a feint. Their swords clacked together, and the audience roared.

"Bion is missing," Hector said, stepping back and swooping his sword around his head.

Kallistos froze. He knew that voice. He moved in close and clashed his sword against Hector's. "Alexios," he hissed. "What in Hades are you doing?"

"Saving you," Alexios replied, spinning around and twirling his sword. The crowd stomped and the chorus sang of war and deaths of heroes.

"I don't need your help," Kallistos said, lunging. "You will pay for his death!" he yelled for the crowd.

"Achilles, Achilles, Achilles…" rang through the amphitheater as the crowd stomped and chanted. Kallistos's rage fueled his fight and he wished he were truly Achilles.

He hacked with his wooden sword, marveling at

how light on his feet Alexios was. The sparring was much better than he had choreographed between him and Bion. Emotion took over and, for a moment, the play disappeared.

He'd never been so hurt—so angry—at anyone. Patroclus was the symbol of all he had lost, and Alexios would pay. He swung his sword hard and Alexios hopped out of the way and sprinted to the other side of the stage. The crowd "ooohed" at the nimble move and Kallistos's rage sprang from his chest in a rush of heat.

"He was my friend!" Kallistos yelled.

"And my enemy!"

"You will not go back to your wife, I'll see to that." Kallistos sprang, close to Alexios, and smacked his arm with the sword.

Alexios grabbed him around the neck and pulled him close. "I never meant to hurt you," he said as Kallistos pushed him away.

"You don't abide by your own philosophy," Kallistos said. He ducked his head and barreled into Alexios, knocking him to the ground. Both swords dropped, and the chorus, unsure of the cues for the change in the scene, sang louder.

Kallistos tried to hold down Alexios, but he was so strong underneath him.

"Please, Kallistos," Alexios said. "I started out planning to help Sophocles, but I changed my mind when I realized how wrong it was. I was planning to tell you at the river, but I didn't want you to be upset when performing."

"Yet you chose not to tell me." He straddled Alexios's chest, pinning him. The chorus repeated the battle chant they had already gone through—this time loud and strong.

"I didn't want to lose you."

Kallistos growled. "Why did you agree to help the old man to begin with?" He shoved Alexios' shoulders onto the ground and held him down. The crowd cheered.

Alexios panted. The chorus voices rose. "I was only thinking of myself. I made a mistake and I'm so sorry. I love you."

Kallistos felt a chink in his heart's armor. No, this man had lied to him. Used him. He rolled off him and reached for his sword as Alexios caught him from behind and pushed him face-first onto the ground.

The crowd roared and the chorus belted out their song. A lone drummer beat a steady cadence, the signal that the end was near.

"Sophocles knows and he will make sure I am not

ever on his stage. But I couldn't hurt you. I should have never listened to him—or the call of fame."

Biting back tears, Kallistos tried to pull himself forward on the ground to escape. The chorus chanted, "Kill the traitor, kill him", and the audience took up the chant.

"You should've told me."

"I know. I am so sorry. Let me prove myself. Give me a chance. Give us a chance. I have made a mistake and will never recover from hurting you."

Kallistos's tears returned and great sobs racked him. He had to get control of himself for the sake of his plays and he tried again to squirm out from under Alexios. "Why should I believe you?" he sobbed. "How do I know you aren't still lying? Still vying for glory by taking on the part of Hector—one you did not earn?"

"Kill him," the crowd chanted. The drumbeat picked up its cadence and the chorus sang.

"I'm here now for you. I was leaving town when I saw Stephanos's men searching for Bion. I knew I had to come help you—not let your play be ruined. Diokles gave me the mask and sword and a quick briefing on Hector's part. Why would I do that, if not for you? I knew you were angry."

Kallistos grunted.

"I'll stand at your side as long as you'll allow it," Alexios said. "Now kill me and let's start our life together." The drumbeat quickened to almost a roll and the audience's chants grew louder. "Kill, kill, kill…"

Kallistos's resolve broke in a great rush of emotion. He loved this man—all of him. Men made mistakes. He'd certainly made his own and his life would be miserable without Alexios—he'd relive the tragedy until his death.

Man had the right to make his own choices and live according to his own thoughts. He could make the choice of forgiveness. "I love you too, Alexios," he whispered.

Alexios rolled off him and stood and Kallistos grabbed his sword from the ground and kicked away Hector's.

"Kill him!"

"We will be together forever," Alexios said, holding his hands out.

Kallistos ran at him, stabbing him with the wooden sword in what he hoped would be a show of emotion that would rival anything seen at the festival so far. The drumbeat sped, then the tempo descended.

"Please grant me that you will return my body to

my family," Alexios shouted. He performed Hector well and staggered as if mortally wounded.

"Kill, kill, kill!"

"I will have my revenge!" Kallistos pretended to stab Alexios again and again and Alexios dropped to the ground as if dead, his limbs splayed out and his head to the side—the mask flat on the dirt.

The crowd stomped in approval, roaring as if they watched the great Achilles battle at the gates of Troy.

"He is dead!" Kallistos knelt beside the body of Hector and whispered, "Promise me there will only be truth. No more lies."

"I promise," Alexios whispered. "On my honor."

Kallistos stood and walked around Hector's body. He waved his sword in the air in victory and the chorus sang of the great battle that had been won. The drummer slowed his beat then stopped.

It was time. Kallistos had chosen to change the timeline of events in the Trojan War—and he hoped the crowd would respond favorably. He jumped up on the altar and looked toward the side of the *skene*—guiding the audience's view.

The chorus sang about Odysseus and his travels. From around the *skene*, the Trojan horse appeared—pushed by servants and flanked by Diokles as

Odysseus. The crowd let out a singular awed intake of breath.

"I have a plan to defeat Troy!" Diokles yelled. The horse came to a stop just in front of the *skene*—its colorful halter and saddle painted by the finest painter in Athens.

Kallistos paused, giving the audience time to take in the magnificent prop. The crowd sat in almost total stunned silence. Smoke rose from behind the horse, and Kallistos scowled.

Smoke?

Suddenly, the entire back end of the horse was on fire, with thick black smoke rolling above. The flames spread quickly over the paints and into the horse's rope mane. Diokles backed away, stumbling and falling on his backside.

"What is happening?" Kallistos yelled. Alexios jumped up and ran to him and the audience screamed and laughed.

Hector and Odysseus, fleeing a flaming horse? It must be a sight for the theater. The three men, Achilles, Hector, and Odysseus, hopped up on the altar and watched the great horse burn, arms around each other.

The play was a mockery. Kallistos didn't know whether to laugh or cry at the bizarre turn of events.

The crowd sang drinking songs and watched the great horse burn.

"Did you do this?" Kallistos whispered to Alexios.

"I would never. I promised. Only truth." Alexios stared into Kallistos's eyes.

Kallistos warmed. Of course Alexios didn't start the fire. He came to rescue the plays. He cared. His word proved his bond.

The flames shot high—fortunately the blaze was away from the *skene*—and the smoke billowed. *You could probably see it from Troy*, Kallistos mused.

Men made choices but couldn't control the outcome of things—and that was where faith came in, and optimism. Belief in an intrinsic goodness. Many in the audience stood, trying to get a better glimpse of the blazing horse.

"It's going to be all right," Kallistos said, hugging Alexios. "We have each other. And I have faith in us."

"Bion did this, of that I am sure," Diokles said. "He was out by the horse when I was preparing to come onstage and I didn't get time to ask him where he had been. He must have lit the tail afire. I'm surprised the servants didn't see him."

The smoke spiraled up in a tall cone of black, towering high in the sky. The chorus had run out of song to sing, and joined the men at the altar, waiting on the horse to turn to ash.

Kallistos shook his head. "Some of them were probably helping him. Sophocles's money reaches far." He turned to where Sophocles sat. The old man was gone.

Everything had gone from tragedy to comedy, and it was fine. Kallistos laughed.

EPILOGUE

*A*lexios stood with the chorus as Kallistos accepted the laurel crown from the *archon*. The audience shouted "Kallistos" again and again, and he ducked his head and smiled then lifted his chin before waving. The ashes of the grand horse had been removed overnight and the judges had taken most of the morning to reach their decision on the Dionysia winner.

Kallistos held out his hand for Alexios to join him onstage. Alexios walked out to cheers of "Hector!" Kallistos wrapped his arms around him and pulled him close.

"We won!" Kallistos said. Stephanos beamed beside him. He motioned Diokles to join them.

Stephanos moved over to make room for Diokles.

"I must admit that I am a little surprised the judges picked an unfinished play. But they apparently loved the flaming horse."

"I'll bet Sophocles will use fire next year." Kallistos laughed. "He'll set Athens aflame."

Alexios looked over to Sophocles' seat. It remained empty. The old man didn't have the integrity to face his own loss. It would be pointless to have him prosecuted—they had little proof, and his stature in the community was intact.

"Let him try to burn the city," Alexios said. "He won't win. We'll bring the sea, or the sun and moon, or even the stars. He'll be no match."

"But how?" Kallistos ran his hands through his hair. "How can we triumph again?"

"Do you doubt us? We have strength of mind and character, Beautiful One. Love will prevail. It always does."

Kallistos smiled, and Alexios winked at him and pulled him close. He drew Kallistos into a deep kiss and the crowd stomped its approval. His Beautiful One.

The End

ABOUT THE AUTHOR

USA Today bestselling author Kerry Adrienne loves history, science, music and art. She's a mom to more cats than children and she loves live music, traveling, and staying up all night. Because…vampires. She writes romance (paranormal, m/m, historical, time travel, and more), science fiction, and fantasy. In addition to writing books, she's also a college instructor, artist, costumer, editor, and bad guitar player.

Find out more about Kerry Adrienne here:
Website: http://kerryadrienne.com/
Facebook: https://www.facebook.com/authorkerryadrienne
Twitter: @kerryadrienne

Please sign up for her newsletter here:
https://dl.bookfunnel.com/wq7unoxu41
Monthly contests and news!

ALSO BY KERRY ADRIENNE

Shifter Wars:

Waking the Bear

Pursuing the Bear

Taming the Lion

Claiming His Lioness

DSD (with Lia Davis):

Dragon Undercover

Snowed Undercover

Captain Undercover (2019)

All Mine Series:

Senator, Mine

Druid, Mine

Pharaoh, Mine

All Mine: 1Night Stand Collection

Gallant Gentleman's Guild (G3):

Artist's Touch

Sculptor's Desire

Black Hills Wolves Series (shared world, Decadent Publishing):

The Wolf and the Butterfly

Standalones:

Double Eclipse

Auld Lang Syne

Cruise Control

Storm Damaged

The Guardian of Blackbird Inn

Saving His Wolf

Ghost in a Bottle (with Lia Davis)

First Contact (with Lia Davis)

Anthologies:

Beefcake m/m authors (Artemis Wolffe)

Unconditional Surrender

Box of 1Night Stands: 17 Sizzling Nights

Spring Fever: Shifters in Love

Come Undone: Romance Stories Inspired by the Music of Duran Duran

Wicked: Erotic Paranormal Romance Vol 3

Wicked Legends

Starstruck Holidays: A MM Sci-Fi Holiday Romance Anthology

Mated: A Paranormal Romance Shifter Anthology

Scorched: Thirteen Dragon Shifter Paranormal Romance Standalones